## "Are you and your daughter all right?" Nate asked.

She nodded. "We're fine, but what happened?"

"The guys who followed you are both...taken care of." Nate amended what he was going to say in deference to the little girl. He pushed the door open wider, giving the child a reassuring smile. "Meredith, I need to know what's going on."

She shook her head. "My name isn't Meredith. It's Melissa. Melissa Harris. And we can't stay. We need to get out of here, now. Before anyone else sees us."

Nate knew the woman was Meredith. "Meredith, Melissa, it doesn't matter to me, I remember you from high school and I know very well you remember me, too." He crossed his arms over his chest and planted himself in front of the doorway. "I've wounded two men," he added bluntly. "I'm a sheriff's deputy sworn to uphold the law. I can't just leave."

Meredith actually winced. "I know, and I'm sorry. Of course you can't leave. We'll go on our own. I refuse to put my daughter's life in jeopardy."

Nate glanced down at Hailey. Her tear-stre~~~~ ~~~~ e and the fear reflected ~~~~~~~~~~~~~~~~~~~~~~~~~~~~ his heart.

He closed his eyes ~~~~~~~~~~~~~~~~~~~~~~~~~~~~ going to regret thi~~~

**Laura Scott** is a nurse by day and an author by night. She has always loved romance, reading faith-based books by Grace Livingston Hill in her teenage years. She's thrilled to have published fourteen books for Love Inspired Suspense. She has two adult children and lives in Milwaukee, Wisconsin, with her husband of thirty years. Please visit Laura at laurascottbooks.com, as she loves to hear from her readers.

### Books by Laura Scott

#### Love Inspired Suspense

#### *SWAT: Top Cops*

# HOLIDAY ON THE RUN

## LAURA SCOTT

**HARLEQUIN** LOVE INSPIRED SUSPENSE

Recycling programs
for this product may
not exist in your area.

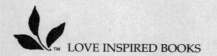

**LOVE INSPIRED BOOKS**

ISBN-13: 978-0-373-44710-7

Holiday on the Run

www.Harlequin.com

**Printed in U.S.A.**

For the Lord is good and His love endures forever;
His faithfulness continues through all generations.
*—Psalms* 100:5

This book is dedicated to all the sisters of my heart, Renee, Marianne, Lisa and Sarah Iding. Love you all and thanks for the great Christmas memories!

# ONE

SWAT team member Nathan Freemont ducked his head against the swirling snow as he jogged across the megamall parking lot to reach the entrance of the building. The place was jam-packed with people, and he knew it was his own fault for waiting until the week before Christmas to do his shopping.

He had only a couple of gifts to buy, one for his dad and another for his dad's new wife, Amelia, so with any luck he could be in and out within thirty minutes. At least, that was his plan. As he was still wearing his uniform, he had no intention of lingering.

Of course, it would help if he had a clue what to buy. He was hoping something in the mall might inspire him.

Nate headed toward the escalator leading up to the second floor, where he could see a shop that specialized in scented lotions. Amelia would probably like something like that, wouldn't she? Didn't all women like that stuff?

He eased through the crowd to step onto the escalator, scanning the sea of faces intensely. He was first and foremost a cop, and he instinctively made sure there wasn't anyone looking suspicious enough to cause trouble.

But he didn't see anyone suspicious. Instead, on the

other side of the escalator, a pretty woman caught his attention. She held the hand of a small girl who he estimated to be about five years old. The woman's features looked familiar, and as they grew closer, his eyes widened in surprise.

"Meredith? Meredith Dupont?" he called above the din.

The woman's head jerked up, her gaze clashing with his, and he noticed her pupils flared in recognition before she deliberately turned her head away, ignoring him.

Was he losing his mind? Hadn't Meredith died years ago? He clearly remembered the devastation he'd felt at the news. He'd even attended her memorial service.

But no matter what his old reality might be, he couldn't seem to tear his gaze away from the woman. As they passed each other, he was convinced he was right. Despite her dark hair, rather than the honey blond he remembered, he knew that the woman was Meredith Dupont. He'd know her anywhere, since he'd fallen in love with her during their senior year of high school.

"Meredith!" he shouted again, louder. She continued to ignore him, and since the escalators were taking them in opposite directions, he made a split-second decision.

He planted his hands on the center area between the set of mechanical stairs and jumped over, prying his way into the crowd. People around him muttered and moved away with annoyance, but he didn't care.

"Meredith!" He dodged around people in an attempt to reach her. "Meredith, wait!"

Meredith swiftly moved farther down the escalator, urging the child along with her. When they reached the ground level, she headed straight into the crowd of adults and children who were waiting in line to see the mall Santa.

Nate followed her, wondering if he was crazy to think the woman was really Meredith, after all. He hadn't seen her in twelve years, since she'd broken his heart by disappearing right after graduation. He'd practically staked out her father's house, begging for information. Her father had claimed she was in rehab and wouldn't provide any details. But her dad had agreed to give Meredith his address.

He'd never heard from her again. And a mere four years later, he'd been told she'd died in a terrible car crash—a result of driving under the influence.

Was it possible he was wrong? No, she'd jerked her head up to look at him when he'd called her name earlier. And her dainty facial features and her wide hazel eyes were exactly as he remembered.

The woman was Meredith. He was sure of it. He zigzagged his way around the display of Santa's elves decorating the North Pole. As he scanned the area again, he noticed two men wearing black leather jackets were also weaving a determined path through the crowd of shoppers toward the area of the mall where Santa was being photographed with children. The tiny hairs on the back of his neck tingled in warning.

Were these two guys actually following Meredith and the little girl? And if so, why?

Nate quickened his pace, dodging around people in an effort to catch up with Meredith. He thought for sure he'd lost her, but then he caught a glimpse of her dark hair above the navy blue parka she'd been wearing. He could see her moving rapidly through the mall, only this time, there was no sign of the little girl.

Surely she hadn't left the child behind?

As much as he wanted to keep an eye out for the two leather-clad guys, he didn't dare take his gaze from Meredith. As he gained ground, she turned back to see if she was being followed and he caught a glimpse of the bulge beneath her jacket.

A flash of admiration made him smile grimly as he realized she was holding the child against her, hiding the girl beneath the bulky winter coat. Smart move, especially since she could dart around shoppers more easily this way.

Meredith was headed toward one of the side exits, and he followed, risking a glance behind him. The two guys in black leather were farther back but still making headway directly toward them.

Nate picked up speed, determined to catch up to her. He no longer needed to confirm she was Meredith. Now it seemed he had to help keep her and the child safe. Her head was averted as he came up alongside.

"This way. We need to ditch the two guys following you," he urged in a low voice.

For a second he thought she would resist, but then she glanced over at him, giving a terse nod.

He tugged at her arm, taking her down a hallway that led to the public restrooms on one side and a staff break room and lockers on the other. He remembered the area all too well from working a mall shooting eighteen months ago.

"Mommy, I'm scared."

"Shh, Hailey, it's okay," Meredith whispered. He could see the very top of the little girl's head poking out from beneath Meredith's parka. "We're fine. Just hang in there a little longer, okay?"

"Through here," he said, pushing open a door that led to the break room.

Meredith had barely got through the doorway when

he heard the distinctive poofing sounds of a gun being fired through a silencer.

"Get down," he shouted, ducking his head and slamming the door behind them, blocking Meredith and her daughter with his body as much as possible.

He pulled his .38 and then dragged Meredith farther back into the locker room. "There's a bathroom up ahead. Get inside and stay low on the floor next to the toilet if you can. Don't come out until I tell you."

Meredith nodded again. Her eyes were frightened, but she was calmer than most women would be under the circumstances. Maybe she didn't realize the extent of the danger, but somehow he didn't think so. No time to consider the implication of that fact now.

Once Meredith and Hailey were safely in the bathroom, he pulled out his cell phone and called for backup, even though he knew it was probably a useless effort. If these guys kept coming, he'd have no choice but to defend himself.

Nate had no idea what he'd stumbled into, but right now, he didn't have time to think about the various possibilities. He grabbed the break room table across from the lockers and flipped it over on its side so that he could use the wide metal slab as a shield.

It wasn't foolproof, but since he wasn't wearing body armor beneath his uniform, it was the best he could do. He hoped that the guys would come in aiming high so he could shoot from his lower position.

He crouched down behind the table, waiting patiently for the gunmen to approach. He couldn't hear a peep from either Meredith or Hailey, which was good.

The doorknob of the break room slowly turned, and he held his pistol steady on the top edge of the table. Nate held his breath, knowing he couldn't shoot until he knew for sure who was on the other side of the door. He didn't dare fire at some innocent mall staff member.

The door swung open, and several long seconds passed before one of the guys in black leather edged around the corner to peer into the room. When he caught a glimpse of the guy's gun, Nate knew the waiting time was over.

"Police! Drop your weapons!" he yelled. When the guy didn't comply, Nate fired off two rounds, one of them lodging in the wooden door frame a fraction of an inch from where the guy's face had been. Instantly, the face disappeared.

Nate swallowed hard and kept his gaze trained on the doorway, knowing his situation was grim. The gunmen had the advantage, not only because there were two of them against one but also because they knew exactly where he was located. Plus, it wasn't exactly as if the metal tabletop was a bulletproof barrier.

But he refused to give up. If he died today, that was fine, but he'd make sure to take these two gunmen with him. He had no idea why these guys were following Meredith and Hailey, but no way would he allow either of them to be hurt.

Nate adjusted his aim, trying to anticipate the gunmen's next move. Seconds passed by with impossible slowness, but he knew the value of patience.

The two men came in with a one-two punch, guns blazing. Nate fired in return, taking the first guy down even as one bullet whistled past his own head, while another plowed through the tabletop, mere inches from Nate's right shoulder. He fired at the second guy, catching him in the upper arm. The gunman cried out in pain and dropped his gun, sliding to the floor with a surprised expression in his eyes.

Nate didn't hesitate, leaping over the table and kicking both of the gunmen's weapons well out of the way before checking to see if they were still alive.

They both were.

The first guy was bleeding from his abdomen, so Nate grabbed some towels and pressed them over the wound. He pulled a chair over, tipping it on its side to add pressure and slow down the bleeding.

The other guy was still conscious, holding his own hand over the wound in his biceps. "You're not going to get away with this," he said in a harsh tone.

"You're the one who fired at a cop," Nate said grimly, even though he had no idea what he'd stumbled into. He quickly cuffed the man to a metal bar beneath the table and then spun on his heel to head back to the bathroom where Meredith was hiding with Hailey. He was stunned to hear singing, catching the phrase "Jesus loves me." The choice surprised him since Meredith hadn't ever been particularly religious in high school.

Obviously things had changed. She not only was alive and had a daughter but also believed in God.

"Meredith? It's me, Nate. Are you and Hailey all right?"

The singing stopped, and he could hear movement inside before the door opened a crack, revealing Meredith's face. "We're fine, but what happened?"

"The guys who followed you are both—taken care of." Nate amended what he was going to say in deference to the little girl. He pushed the bathroom door open wider, giving Hailey a reassuring smile. "The bad guys are going to be arrested so they can't hurt you anymore. I have backup and an ambulance on the way. Meredith, I need to know what's going on."

She shook her head. "My name isn't Meredith. It's

Melissa. Melissa Harris. And we can't stay. We need to get out of here, now. Before anyone else sees us."

Nate knew the woman was Meredith, and the name Melissa wasn't that much different. She'd obviously changed it, but for the life of him he didn't know why. "Meredith—Melissa, your name doesn't matter to me. I remember you from high school, and I know very well you remember me, too." He crossed his arms over his chest and planted himself in front of the bathroom doorway. "You're not leaving. Not until you tell me what's going on."

Her gaze implored him to listen to reason. "Please let us go. Making me talk to the police will only put us in more danger."

Nate stared at her, trying to understand what was going on. "I've wounded two men," he said bluntly. "I'm a sheriff's deputy sworn to uphold the law. I can't just leave."

Melissa actually winced. "I know, and I'm sorry. Of course you can't leave. We'll go on our own. You have to trust me on this, Nate. I refuse to put my daughter's life in jeopardy."

Nate glanced down at Hailey. Her tear-streaked face and the fear reflected in her hazel gaze ripped a hole in his heart.

He closed his eyes and sighed, knowing he was likely going to regret this. "Okay, let's get out of here. I'm coming with you."

Melissa's eyes widened in surprise. "Where?"

"If you think I'm letting you go off on your own, you're nuts. You have two choices. Stay here and wait for my backup or allow me to take you someplace safe."

She hesitated and then reluctantly nodded. "Okay. We'll go with you, for now."

He planned to stick with her longer than *for now*, but there wasn't time to argue. His team would be here at any second.

His boss, Griff, would likely fire him for leaving the scene of a police shooting, but there wasn't anything he could do about that now. Not when the fear he saw in Melissa was too real. No way was he going to put a woman and her child in danger.

And he was determined to get to the bottom of whatever Melissa was involved in.

Melissa couldn't believe that out of all the people to stumble across in Milwaukee, Wisconsin, it would be Nate Freemont.

Her old high school sweetheart.

The man she'd been forced to leave behind.

She wasn't totally surprised to find out he was a cop, since law enforcement was all he'd talked about back when they were in school. Twelve years later, fate, or maybe God, had brought them back together. Being with a cop was dangerous, and she told herself that after he'd helped her get away, she'd ditch Nate as soon as she could.

Deep down, she was relieved not to be alone. Hailey didn't deserve to be in danger like this. Melissa knew coming home to see her father in the hospital before he passed away had been a mistake. She'd thought for sure everyone around here believed her dead and buried.

Apparently not. Something she should have been prepared for, since after all, there was no statute of limitations on murder. Despite the fact that she'd changed her identity and faked her death, they'd found her. She'd noticed a tail on her as soon as she'd left the hospital, so she'd come to the busy megamall, trying to disappear into the crowd of people. Her intent had been to hop a bus, but Nate had shown up before she'd been able to make her way back outside.

And then he'd solved the problem by taking down the two men who'd followed her.

She picked up Hailey and followed Nate out of the break room, glancing at the two men who lay wounded. She shivered, feeling sick at the thought of what might have happened if Nate hadn't seen her and recognized her. Granted, hearing him call her by her birth name had been a shock. But she might not have escaped the gunmen if not for Nate's help. She'd prayed for him while she and Hailey had hidden in the bathroom singing church songs.

"This way," Nate said, gesturing over to the right. There was a long hallway that ended with a door marked Exit. She took Hailey's hand and headed down the hall.

"Mommy, I'm hungry," Hailey whined.

"I know, sweetheart. We'll get something to eat soon," she said, trying to soothe her daughter.

Nate nodded, and when he smiled, he reminded her so much of the young man she'd fallen for all those years ago. "We'll get something to eat, but first we need to get to my car, okay?"

Hailey gazed up at Nate with big solemn hazel eyes, and Melissa's heart squeezed in her chest at the hero worship she saw reflected there. Hailey was too young to remember her own father, who'd died before she was even born. It was only logical that she'd latch on to Nate as a father figure, especially after he'd saved their lives.

"We're going to have to walk in the snow," Nate said, his tone apologetic as he gestured to the heavy metal door leading outside. "I'm parked way on the other side of the mall."

"No problem," Melissa said. She didn't want to go anywhere near her rusty old sedan, even though it had cost her dearly—five hundred in cash. The gunmen had followed her from the hospital, which meant her license plate number was compromised. For all she knew, they'd already reported the information to whoever was paying them.

She tried not to give in to the wave of hopelessness. She would not only have to escape from Nate but also need to find a new vehicle. She didn't have enough money to buy another car, so she'd be forced to take a series of buses to their next destination. Wherever that might be.

Nate pushed open the door and gestured for her and Hailey to go out first. A blast of cold air hit her in the face, stealing her breath. Melissa bent over to tie Hailey's scarf over her daughter's nose and mouth.

"It might be better if I carry her," Nate said in a low voice. "We'll get to my car faster that way."

She nodded, knowing he was right. "Hailey? This is my friend, Nate. He's going to carry you to the car, okay?"

"Okay," Hailey agreed.

Under normal circumstances, Melissa wouldn't have been at all happy to know her daughter was willing to let a stranger carry her. But nothing about this trip back to Milwaukee was normal. She wished she'd made a different decision, but it was too late to go back and change the past. After all this time, it should have been safe enough to fulfill her father's dying wish to see his only grandchild.

But it wasn't. The only thing she could do now was to disappear again, creating new identities for herself and Hailey.

Melissa quickened her pace to keep up with Nate's long strides as they made their way through the snow-covered parking lot. She hadn't seen snow like this in years, although Hailey had been thrilled with the idea of having a white Christmas. Thankfully the snow had stopped, but the ground was still slippery.

A half dozen police cars were parked around the entrance to the mall where she'd come into the building, and her heart leaped into her throat. Was the dirty cop there right now? Pretending to be one of the good guys?

Nate didn't glance over at the police cars, leading the way to the furthest part of the parking lot.

When they reached the vehicle, she remembered Hailey's booster seat.

"Hailey will have to ride in the back," she said as Nate opened the passenger-side door. "Her car seat is still in my car, along with our suitcase."

"We'll pick them up," Nate assured her.

"Thanks." Melissa scooted into the backseat beside Hailey, while Nate slid behind the wheel. He started the car and then went back outside to brush off the light covering of snow.

She shivered, trying to remember where she'd left her car. Not far from here, she recalled, but near the area where the police cars were gathered. The thought of going any closer filled her with dread.

Should she forget about the child safety seat and their meager belongings? She'd rather not, since the lack of a booster chair could get them pulled over. Either way, it would bring her too close to the police for comfort.

"All set?" Nate asked as he came back into the car.

"Yes." She forced herself to sound more confident than she felt. "I parked three rows over, closer to the building."

"Okay." Nate backed out of the parking space and followed her directions. She huddled beside Hailey as the red-and-blue lights flashed around them.

"There—the tan sedan parked beside the white pickup truck." She pulled the keys out of her purse, which was slung across her chest beneath her coat, and handed them to Nate.

Within five minutes, Nate had their suitcase stored in his trunk and the booster seat secured in the backseat with Hailey belted in. Melissa chose to stay in the back with her daughter, but Nate didn't object.

It wasn't until they left the mall parking lot that she was able to breathe easier. It was a huge relief to know that she and Hailey were safe, from both the gunmen and the police.

Well, except for Nate.

The sick feeling in her stomach returned with a vengeance. Nate was a good guy, and she knew that he'd put his career on the line to help them.

Yet he was the last person she could trust with her secret. He couldn't know the reason she'd run away from Milwaukee days after their high school graduation twelve years ago.

The same reason she remained a target all these years later. All because she'd witnessed something she shouldn't have seen. Corruption of local politics as well as local law enforcement.

Dragging Nate into this mess would only hurt him and damage his reputation beyond repair in the long run. The best thing she could do for him was to disappear once and for all.

Never to be heard from again.

# TWO

Nate kept an eye on Melissa using the rearview mirror. Her face was pale, her expression strained. He squelched a flash of empathy. Granted, she and Hailey had been through a lot, but he wasn't about to let her off the hook, not by a long shot. The minute Melissa and Hailey were safe, he was going to get the answers he needed about what was going on.

Leaving the scene of the crime after he'd shot and wounded two men, even in self-defense, was the hardest thing he'd ever done. Doubt battered his conscience as he drove through the darkness of night.

What did he really know about Melissa after all these years? Obviously she wasn't the same girl he'd fallen for in high school. For all he knew, Melissa could be mixed up in all sorts of things now, even something criminal.

Yet he'd risked everything by leaving with her. What on earth had he been thinking?

"Mommy, I'm hungry," Hailey said, her tone plaintive.

He'd almost forgotten his promise to feed the little girl. He gestured through the windshield. "There's a fast-food restaurant up ahead. Do you want me to go into the drive-through?"

"Yes, please," Melissa said, reaching over to put her hand on her daughter's arm. "Would you like some chicken bites?"

Hailey's head bobbed up and down. "Yay! Chicken bites!"

Despite the seriousness of the situation, Nate found himself smiling at the child's enthusiasm. And the truth hit him like a fist to the solar plexus. The real reason he'd left the scene of the crime was for Hailey's safety. The little girl didn't deserve to be dragged into danger, to be chased by men with guns.

Hailey was the true innocent in all of this. And he was determined to do whatever was necessary to keep the child safe from harm.

He pulled into the drive-through lane and waited in line for their turn. "Chicken bites for Hailey. What do you want, Mer—uh, Melissa? And what would you like to drink?"

"I'll have a cheeseburger and water. Milk for Hailey, please." She dug in her pocket for money, but he frowned and shook his head, waving it away.

Nate ordered a cheeseburger for himself, too, before pulling up to the next window to pay. When they were given their food, he handed the bag back to Melissa.

"Thank you," she said softly. "Here's your sandwich," she added, handing up his wrapped burger.

"No problem." He pulled over to park so he could eat. He listened while Melissa assisted Hailey with her chicken bites, encouraging the little girl to drink her milk.

He couldn't deny Melissa was an attentive mother. Was she putting on an act for his benefit? He didn't think so. But just caring about her daughter didn't necessarily mean she was completely innocent in whatever had caused the two men to follow her through the mall. As much as he wanted to believe she wasn't a criminal, he knew better than most that power and greed could turn the most innocent to a life of crime.

And he was determined to get to the bottom of whatever she'd got herself involved in.

"Why did you disappear after graduation?" he asked.

Melissa didn't say anything for a long moment. "I'd rather not talk about this right now, Nate," she murmured in a low voice, tipping her head toward Hailey.

He drew in a ragged breath, fighting his frustration. He understood that she wanted to protect her daughter from whatever had happened back then. Or from whatever caused her to run away now. Still, he couldn't help feeling as if she had no intention of cooperating with him, despite the fact that he'd risked his career for her.

Shot two men to keep them safe.

Nate forced himself to finish his burger, which tasted like sawdust on his tongue. He'd find a motel room for Melissa and Hailey to stay in for tonight, but he wasn't about to let them out of his sight.

Not until he found out who she was running from and why.

Melissa wasn't hungry but knew she needed to eat to keep up her strength. The grief of her father's impending death, which she'd pushed into the background when faced with the threat of danger, returned full force, making her throat swell with repressed tears.

A wave of fury filled her chest, and she had to make herself let go of her anger at the unfairness of it all. Since when was life fair? Right from the beginning, she'd been an innocent bystander. In the wrong place at the wrong time.

Hadn't she suffered enough? She'd lost her home and her life, not to mention Nate. She'd started over in a new place with a new identity, not just once but twice. Thankfully she'd been able to find enough work to support herself—work she could do primarily at home with a computer. But still, it wasn't as if designing websites and doing freelance graphic art work would have been her first career choice.

And surely her daughter deserved a better life?

The very idea of going back on the run, starting over and changing their identities again, filled her with despair. Her father had helped finance her new life twelve years ago.

But this time she was on her own.

Melissa closed her eyes, silently praying for strength and for safety. When she opened them, she was disconcerted to find Nate turned in his seat, staring at her.

For a moment her mind flashed back to the last time she'd seen Nate. The night of their graduation, when he'd kissed her beneath the oak tree in her backyard.

The night before her world had turned upside down.

If only she could go back to change the sequence of events. But those kinds of thoughts were useless. Better to concentrate on moving forward. She needed to stay focused on sheltering Hailey by doing what needed to be done.

"Are you ready to go?" Nate asked, breaking the silence.

"Sure. Finish your milk, Hailey," she said, turning toward her daughter.

"Okay, Mommy." Hailey drained the last of her milk with a loud slurp through her straw, making Melissa smile. "All done."

She bagged up the trash and passed it up to Nate.

Would he go outside to dispose of their trash? And if so, did she have the guts to steal his car, drive off and leave him behind?

Thankfully, he took the decision out of her hands by simply setting the bag aside and pulling out of the restaurant parking lot.

Melissa didn't want to steal a car, anyway, especially not Nate's, but what else could she do? Asking Nate to take her to the bus stop would be futile. He'd already insisted on taking her to a motel, and once Hailey was settled for the night, she wouldn't be able to continue avoiding his questions.

Nate had had a strong stubborn streak even back when they were dating in high school, and she doubted that trait would have faded over time. Especially now that he was a cop.

She needed to find some way to convince him to let her go without him knowing the details that had the power to hurt him.

Far more than she'd hurt him already.

"Wait. Where are you going?" she asked in alarm when she realized he'd made a U-turn to head back toward the shopping mall. Even from this distance, she could still see the red-and-blue flashing lights from the police cars gathered outside the mall entrance.

No doubt there were officers searching for her. And she didn't want to think about what would happen if they found her. Hadn't they already tarnished her reputation? If they used the same tactics again, she could lose custody of her daughter.

Hailey would be the one to suffer, another innocent bystander in a political web of deceit and lies.

"Relax. There's a motel not far from here called the

Forty Winks Motel," Nate assured her. "We'll stay there tonight. They have several adjoining rooms."

Adjoining rooms? She tried to hide her dismay. Did that mean Nate was planning to stay all night, too? If that was his intent, it would be difficult for her and Hailey to sneak away.

Difficult, but hopefully not impossible.

She refused to consider failure an option.

Melissa held her breath as Nate drove past the mall and turned left onto a side street. Her chest was tight with tension, and even after he pulled into the motel parking lot, she couldn't seem to relax.

They weren't far enough away from the mall—or the hospital, for that matter—for her peace of mind.

Then again, Melissa was certain she wouldn't find peace until she left the Milwaukee area forever. And this time, once she left, she wouldn't look back.

"This doesn't appear to be the type of place to take cash," she said, digging into her jeans pocket as he parked near the lobby entrance. "We'd be better off driving out a ways. The smaller motels aren't as picky about payment."

Nate turned around in his seat. "One of the reasons I wanted to come here is that they're cop-friendly. All I need to do is to show them my badge and they'll take cash."

She smiled through her trepidation and dug in her pocket for the small wad of bills she'd tucked there. "All right. I have my share." Now that they were here at the motel, she wondered about his personal life. "So, uh, are you sure your girlfriend won't mind?"

He lifted a brow. "No wife, no girlfriend," he said lightly.

The news shouldn't have been reassuring, yet she couldn't squash the brief flash of relief.

When she held out the cash, Nate scowled and shook his head. "Keep your money. I'll take care of this."

Before she could argue, he pushed open the driver's side door, letting in a blast of cold air. When he shut the door behind him, she couldn't help watching him as he walked into the building. Not that she was interested in picking up where they'd left off twelve years ago, but it was surprising to realize just how much taller and broader across the shoulders Nate had become.

Melissa tore her gaze away, glancing over to make sure Hailey was all right. Her daughter's eyelids were drooping. No doubt she would fall asleep as soon as they were inside their motel room.

Melissa told herself that it was a good thing, since Hailey needed her rest. They'd been on the move for the past two days, making the trip from South Carolina up to Wisconsin. The moment they'd arrived in Milwaukee, Melissa had called the hospital, only to discover her father had taken a turn for the worse. She'd headed straight over, despite the fact that Hailey had been travel-weary from the long car ride.

She'd been happy to see that her father was still conscious, that he'd smiled at her and seemed so happy at meeting his granddaughter in person for the first time. Oh, sure, they'd been using Skype to keep in touch, but it wasn't the same.

Within five minutes of leaving the hospital, she'd noticed the tail. Two men in a dark car, keeping pace behind her. She'd tried to lose them, taking a turn into the mall parking lot and quickly parking the car to dart into the building.

Where Nate had recognized her, despite the fact that it

had been twelve years and she'd changed her hair color. Unable to master the art of wearing tinted contacts, she hadn't been able to do much more to change her appearance.

She was so completely lost in her thoughts that she didn't hear Nate return until he slammed the trunk, the noise making her startle.

He opened the passenger-side door closest to Hailey. "I have your suitcase. Can you carry Hailey?"

"Of course," she said, pasting a smile on her face.

"I wanna walk," Hailey said in an abrupt flash of independence.

"Okay, that's fine," Melissa assured her. She disconnected the lap strap, allowing Hailey to climb down from the seat onto the slush-covered parking lot. She edged around the seat to follow Hailey, disconcerted when her daughter skipped alongside Nate.

"We stayed in lotsa hotels on the way here, right, Mommy?" Hailey said, her previous sleepiness seeming to have vanished. "Do they have the kids' channel here?"

"I'm sure they do," Nate assured her, holding the door open for them so they could precede him into the building. "Our rooms are on the second floor," he said, leading the way up the stairs. "We're in 210 and 212."

Melissa nodded, moving slowly enough to match Hailey's small steps climbing the stairs. As they made their way down the hall, she watched the numbers outside the doors until they arrived at the correct ones. Nate didn't hand her a key, though. He simply unlocked a door and held it open for her.

"Thanks," she murmured, glancing around the room to locate the connecting door.

Nate set her suitcase down on the bed and then placed the key card on the dresser. "I'd appreciate it if you'd keep the connecting door between our rooms unlocked," he said as he crossed over to it and opened it.

"I understand," she said evasively, unwilling to make a promise she might not be able to keep.

"Movie, Mommy! Check and see if there's a children's movie that I can watch."

Since Hailey didn't look sleepy anymore, Melissa obliged by picking up the remote and flipping through the channels until she found the one Hailey wanted.

Nate left, presumably to go to his own room. A few minutes later, he opened his side of the connecting door.

"It's time we talked," he said in a low voice. "Hailey will be fine here, watching her show. We'll leave the connecting doors open in case she needs something."

Melissa wanted to protest, but of course there wasn't a rationale for putting this discussion off any longer.

As she followed him into his room, she tried to figure out how much she could safely tell him. He needed just enough information to understand the level of danger.

Including a good reason to let her go.

Full of apprehension, she dropped into a seat next to the small round table tucked in the corner of his room. Her heart was beating too fast, and she took several deep breaths in order to bring her pulse down.

"Who were those men following you?" Nate asked, his tone soft but firm.

"I don't know," she answered honestly. "I've never seen either of them before in my life."

Nate's mouth thinned as if he wasn't sure he believed her. "Okay, then why were they following you?"

"I don't know that, either," she said. When his face tightened in anger, she knew she'd have to tell him something. "Listen, Nate, you need to understand, all of this started a long time ago."

He folded his arms over his chest. "I'm listening."

She licked her suddenly dry lips. "You remember how I waitressed at the restaurant back in high school, right?"

Nate nodded. "At El Matador, which is still there, believe it or not."

Still in Brookmont, the elite suburb of Milwaukee that she and Nate had once called home.

The thought of the upscale restaurant being there all these years later was not reassuring. Did it continue to be a meeting point for the upper echelon of Brookmont? Or had they moved their little clique somewhere different after that fateful night?

"Melissa, what happened back then? What caused you to move away and change your name?" Nate asked.

"Something terrible occurred the night after graduation," she said.

Nate nodded slowly. "Go on," he encouraged her.

She couldn't for the life of her find the words to explain in a way that didn't give away the entire truth. The silence stretched painfully long between them.

"I heard about the drugs that were found in your room," Nate finally said. "I didn't want to believe that you were an addict, but your father admitted that he sent you to rehab."

She snapped her head up to stare at Nate. "You believed that?" she asked in an agonized whisper. "Even though we spent every free moment we could together, you still believed that?"

"You weren't here to tell me otherwise," Nate said, accusation lacing his tone. "What was I supposed to think? You disappeared and I never heard from you again, not one letter in response to all the ones I sent you."

She blinked in surprise. "What letters?"

Nate's gaze narrowed. "The letters I gave your father

to send to you. He wouldn't give me your address, but he agreed to send you my letters. I kept waiting and waiting to hear back from you, but I never did."

Melissa's entire body went numb, as if someone had dumped a bucket of ice water over her head. "I'm sorry," she murmured. "I'm so sorry."

"For what?" Nate challenged her. "For leaving without saying goodbye? For not even trying to get in touch with me? I commuted to college my first year because I was afraid you wouldn't find me when you came back. But you never did."

The anguish in Nate's voice lashed at her like a whip. It wasn't her fault that she'd been forced to leave, but he'd been deeply hurt by her actions nonetheless. And why hadn't her father passed along his letters? Had her father been afraid that Nate would come after her?

Looking at Nate now, she knew that was exactly what he would have done.

"Well?" he demanded in a harsh tone.

She glanced over her shoulder at the open connecting door between their rooms. "Not so loud, or Hailey will hear."

Nate's jaw tightened with anger, and she knew that there was no way of getting around the fact that he needed to hear a portion of her story.

"I was working at the restaurant the night after graduation. In fact, I was scheduled to close. It was pretty busy. The place was packed, but as the hour grew later, there were only a few tables left. A group at one table in particular lingered, so I was trying to get as much of the cleanup work done as possible." She paused, shivering at the memory of what transpired that night.

"Go on," Nate urged.

"I cleaned out the large coffeepots in the back room,

and then I hauled some garbage out to the dumpsters. Usually the dishwasher does that, but he was busy, and I was anxious to leave."

"To meet me," Nate said in a quiet voice.

She bit her lip and nodded, remembering the plans they'd made long ago. "Yes, to meet you."

"So what stopped you from coming?"

"I couldn't lift the garbage bag, so I set it against the Dumpster and was about to go back inside when I heard raised voices. The Dumpster was located not far from the alley, so I went over to investigate. The yelling grew louder, and I should have left. To this day, I wish I had followed my instinct to run away."

Nate's expression grew grim. "What did you see?"

"Five men arguing. I recognized them from the restaurant. They were the ones who had been lingering at the table in my section. In fact, I'd waited on them. I was trying to figure out why they were hanging around when one of the men pulled out a knife and stabbed the guy across from him in the stomach. I was so surprised, I didn't move. Even after he fell to the ground, blood pooling beneath him, I still didn't really understand what had happened. Not until the man with the knife happened to glance in my direction." Melissa drew in a harsh breath and forced herself to meet Nate's gaze. "That's when I knew that he'd recognized me."

Nate stared at her in horror. "Are you saying you witnessed a murder?"

She nodded slowly. "Yes, that's exactly what I'm saying. And I think it's obvious that the man responsible is determined to silence me once and for all."

# THREE

Unbelievable. Nate stared at Melissa, stunned by her revelation. He'd imagined dozens of scenarios in the long months after she'd disappeared, but never anything remotely like what she'd just described.

Yet even knowing that she'd witnessed a murder didn't explain everything. Why had she decided simply to disappear? Why hadn't she called the police for help? Or talked to him about what she'd seen?

"And the drugs that were found in your bedroom?" he forced himself to ask.

"Planted, as a way to discredit me." Melissa's expression was full of hurt. "A ploy that worked, since you fell for it just like everyone else probably did."

Nate couldn't ignore the flash of guilt. Twelve years ago, he hadn't wanted to believe the girl he'd loved had been a secret addict, but what else was he to think when her father had looked him straight in the eye and explained that she'd been sent to rehab? It wasn't as if he'd had any other theory to explain what had happened.

"You really wrote me letters?" she asked, her tone hesitant.

He nodded slowly. "At least a dozen of them," he admitted. "I didn't realize your father hated me so much that he wouldn't pass them along to you."

Melissa frowned and shook her head. "It wasn't like that, Nate. My father didn't hate you. He was determined to keep me safe, that's all. I'm sure he was afraid that if he gave me your letters, we'd find a way to get back together."

Since that was true, at least on his part, he couldn't argue. Besides, all of that was in the past. He needed to keep focused on the present. Although wrapping his mind around the idea that the men who'd followed Melissa had, in fact, intended to kill her wasn't easy.

"Okay, tell me about these five men," Nate said. "You mentioned at the mall that you couldn't go to the police without risking your and Hailey's lives, which makes me think one of them must be a cop."

Melissa didn't meet his gaze, and the way she twisted her fingers in her lap made him wonder if she was trying to find a way to avoid the truth.

"Listen, you have to tell me what you know," Nate urged. "Otherwise I won't have any choice but to call my boss and have you taken in for questioning."

Her head jerked up, her stormy gaze clashing with his. "Don't," she said sharply. "Hailey will be the one to suffer if you do that."

Nate wanted to yank out his hair in frustration. "Then cooperate with me. What do you know about the five men you saw twelve years ago?"

She hesitated and then let out a heavy sigh. "You were right. One of them was a cop," she confirmed. "I saw him come in several times in uniform, although he wasn't wearing it the night of the murder."

"Do you know his name?" Nate demanded. "Can you describe him?" He didn't like believing a cop had gone bad, but unfortunately it wasn't the first time that one had succumbed to temptation. And probably wouldn't be the last, either.

"I don't know his name," Melissa said. "I wish I did. And he wasn't the one who actually committed murder, but he was there watching the whole thing."

"Party to the crime," Nate muttered. "And could easily be arrested as an accomplice."

"Yes, I'm sure he could. And I think he must have other cops who are willing to bend the rules, too. Otherwise, how would they have got away with stashing drugs in my bedroom?"

Nate could see her point. "Did you find them? Is that why you left?"

Melissa bit her lower lip, another sign of nervousness. "No, I didn't find the drugs. I was too afraid to go home. I ran away and hid until morning, catching a bus when the early route started."

"I don't understand why you didn't come to me for help." Nate knew it was ridiculous to be wounded by actions she'd taken twelve years ago, but he couldn't seem to help himself. "Especially when you knew I was planning to major in criminal justice."

"I didn't want to drag you down with me," she murmured. "I found out from my father that the police showed up on our doorstep first thing in the morning, demanding to speak with me about a stabbing victim found outside the restaurant. My dad thought I was in my room, so he let them in."

"Without a warrant?" Nate asked in dismay.

She nodded. "My dad was shocked to realize I wasn't home. And when the police searched my room and found the drugs, he wasn't sure what was going on. Don't you see? They would have tried to discredit you, too."

"Maybe, or maybe I would have been a credible witness on your behalf," he said grimly.

"I wasn't going to take that chance," she said firmly.

Nate didn't agree with her decision, but there was nothing he could do now to change the past. If he'd paid more attention back then he might have connected the stabbing victim with Melissa's disappearance. But he hadn't. For now, he needed to stay focused on the present. "You must know at least one of the men's names," he said. "You told me you waited on their table. Surely you noticed a name on a credit or debit card?"

"No credit cards. They always paid in cash."

Nate couldn't believe Melissa didn't have a clue to the identity of at least one of the men. "There must be something you remember about these guys. Did they have any scars? Tattoos? Any distinguishing features at all?"

Melissa shook her head, spreading her hands in a gesture of surrender. "I'm sorry, but there's nothing that stands out in my memory."

Nate stared up at the ceiling for a moment, trying to push back the wave of helplessness. "Okay, so you've told me what happened all those years ago, but what about today? How was it that these two guys found you?"

"I noticed the tail as soon as I left the hospital," Melissa said in a low tone.

"Hospital? What were you doing there?"

She blinked rapidly, and Nate was disconcerted to realize she was on the verge of tears. "Visiting my father. His dying wish was to see his granddaughter in person."

The anger he'd felt toward Melissa's father for keeping them apart instantly evaporated. "I'm so sorry," he said huskily.

Melissa sniffed and wiped at her eyes. "Me, too. I honestly didn't think coming home after all this time was that much of a risk. Especially since my father and I faked my death."

"Why did you wait four years to do that?" Nate asked.

"Because they found me in California. So I conveniently died and moved all the way across the country to a new location, with another new name."

Nate couldn't help sympathizing with her. He'd hated the idea that she'd been forced to go on the run, not just once but twice. "Go on. So, you left the hospital and noticed what?"

"I was being followed, so I headed into the mall, hoping to lose them in the crowd."

"Carrying Hailey beneath your winter coat was a smart move," Nate told her.

A slight smile tipped the corner of her mouth. "Thanks. Anyway, from there you know the rest."

Yeah, he knew the rest. The men with guns had shot at him, and he'd shot at them in self-defense. Then he'd left the scene of the crime.

Too bad he didn't have a clue what their next steps should be. He wanted to keep Melissa and Hailey out of harm's way, but right now, he didn't even know who the bad guys were.

"Excuse me. I need to check on Hailey." Melissa rose to her feet and quickly made her way into the other room.

Nate hovered in the doorway between their connecting rooms, listening as she coaxed Hailey into brushing her teeth and putting on her pajamas.

Then the little girl insisted on saying her nighttime prayers.

"God bless Daddy up in Heaven, and Mommy, and Mr. Nate, who saved us today. Amen."

"Amen," Melissa echoed. "Sleep tight, Hailey. I'll be right here if you need anything."

"Okay, Mommy," the little girl murmured sleepily.

Nate was touched by the fact that Hailey had included him in her nighttime prayers.

There were so many things that were different about the woman Melissa was today compared with the girl he'd loved years ago. Yes, she was a mother now, but that wasn't the only thing that had changed.

She was raising her daughter as a Christian. Because of Hailey's father? Did she love him still, even though he'd passed away?

Not that Melissa's feelings were any of his business. He wouldn't risk getting emotionally involved. And not just because he sensed she was still holding something back from him.

She'd left him without a word, breaking his young heart.

No way was he willing to risk another heartbreak.

Melissa took her time getting ready for bed, admittedly as a way to avoid spending more time with Nate.

She'd already told him far more than she'd intended. Anything else would only hurt him.

Closing her eyes for a moment, she mourned what they'd lost. Their young love, so pure, so sweet. They'd never done anything more than kiss, but even twelve years later, she could still remember the sweetness they'd shared. For several weeks after she'd left, she'd find herself looking for him, wishing he was still there for her to lean on.

Why hadn't her father mentioned the letters Nate had written? Surely he hadn't thrown them away. Why not pass them along, especially after she'd been forced to fake her death? They'd both thought she was relatively safe from that point forward.

And where were Nate's letters now? Hidden somewhere in her father's house?

For a moment, she actually considered going back

to the house where she grew up to search for them. But of course, she couldn't take the risk. For one thing, she was pretty sure her dad's house was being watched, the same way the hospital had been. How else had they found her? Besides, heading there was probably exactly what they'd expect her to do.

No, going to her childhood home wasn't an option. Besides, whatever Nate had written hardly mattered now. She'd been married all too briefly before losing her husband to a rare infection that had settled in his lungs. Jeremy had helped her find God and had given her Hailey, the two greatest gifts of all. No reason to go back and attempt to recapture the past.

Far more important to plan the next steps of her mission to keep Hailey safe.

By the time Melissa emerged from the bathroom, Nate's room was dark except for the blue glow of the television. Relieved that she didn't have to talk to him anymore, she slid into the bed next to Hailey. Wearing her jeans and sweater wasn't exactly comfortable, but she didn't plan on sleeping.

Once Nate fell asleep, she'd take Hailey and slip away. Hopefully he wouldn't notice they were gone until morning.

Yet, in spite of herself, Melissa dozed, jerking awake a few hours later. She took a moment to orient herself before sliding out of bed.

Moving silently, she eased toward the doorway between their connecting rooms. The television was off now, and she stood for what seemed like endless moments listening to Nate's deep, rhythmic breathing.

It was tempting to venture into his room to search for his car keys, but she didn't want to risk waking him.

No, her best chance to escape was to slip away without making any noise.

She gently closed the door on her side of the room, hoping to muffle any errant sounds. She packed the few meager belongings they had back into the suitcase and then took out her mobile phone.

Only twenty percent of battery left, but enough juice to enable her to call for a taxi once she was far enough away from the motel.

After setting the suitcase near the door, she went over to the bed to wake Hailey. This would be the most difficult part of sneaking away. If Hailey cried or made any noise at all, she knew Nate would be up in a flash to see what was wrong.

Thankfully, the little girl was so sleepy, she simply curled up against Melissa's chest, snuggling into the hollow of her shoulder.

Since the hallway outside their rooms was heated, she decided to wait until they were safely away before putting Hailey's coat, hat and boots on. Carrying everything with her wasn't easy, but she managed to open the door, wincing when it creaked a bit.

Moving as quickly and silently as possible, she stepped out and then closed the door behind her. The hallway was brightly lit, making it easy to navigate as she headed toward the stairs on the far side of the building, opposite from the lobby.

Inside the stairwell, she paused to get Hailey into her winter gear. She was still half-asleep, so Melissa couldn't exactly make her stand to get dressed. Somehow she slipped her daughter's arms into the coat sleeves. Getting her hat on was no problem, although the boots were difficult. She hoped they wouldn't fall off.

She carried Hailey and the suitcase down the stairs,

and when she reached the bottom, she paused to catch her breath.

Melissa hated the thought of leaving Nate for a second time without saying goodbye, but she forced herself to go anyway. The cold winter air stole her breath as she went outside, and Hailey instantly started crying.

"Shh, it's okay. We're going to be fine."

"It's cold," her daughter sobbed.

"I know, sweetie. We'll get someplace warm soon." Hailey wasn't used to northern winters, having spent her entire life in South Carolina. And the idea of snow was more fun than the cold reality of it.

Melissa stayed alongside the shelter of the building as long as possible before making her way toward the sidewalk. There was a gas station on the other side of the street, but the windows were dark, indicating the place was closed.

Headlights cut through the darkness, heading in her direction. For a moment she froze, fearing she'd been found. But she sighed in relief as the vehicle kept going.

She carefully walked across the slippery surface of the gas station parking lot, wondering if venturing out like this was such a good idea. Would she manage to find a taxi this late? She fumbled for her phone, intending to search for a local car service.

Another pair of headlights approached, only this time, they abruptly turned into the gas station rather than driving past. Melissa froze in the center of the bright lights, her heart lodging in her throat as the car came to an abrupt stop. The driver's side door opened, and a tall figure stepped out.

Survival instincts kicked in, and she dropped the suitcase and turned to run. But she quickly lost her footing on the slippery, snow-covered pavement. She felt herself falling and twisted as much as possible, landing on her shoulder in an attempt to avoid landing on her daughter.

She tried to scramble to her feet, but the driver of the car was on her too quickly, preventing her escape. In the dim recesses of her mind she realized Hailey was crying, but her gaze was focused on the man looming over her.

"Now I've got you," he said with savage satisfaction. He reached down and roughly grabbed her arm as if to yank her to her feet.

No! Melissa kicked at the stranger, screaming for help. She tried to jerk from his grasp, but he held on tight. She let go of Hailey. "Run, Hailey! Run!"

Something hard hit her in the face and she bit back a cry of pain, tears springing to her eyes. At the moment all she cared about was giving Hailey time to get away.

Desperate, she kicked at her captor again.

Out of nowhere, a second figure came out of the darkness, grabbing the man around the throat and dragging him off her. At first she didn't understand what was happening, but then she recognized Nate.

She pushed herself to her feet, taking off after Hailey, scooping her daughter into her arms. Still slipping and sliding, she made her way behind the shelter of the gas station building. As much as she wanted to help Nate take down the guy who'd grabbed her, she knew her priority had to be keeping Hailey away from harm.

Resting against the building, breathing heavily, she closed her eyes and thanked God for sparing them.

"Melissa?" Nate's deep voice cut through the darkness.

"Here," she managed in a low tone.

"Are you all right?" he asked, coming over to where she was huddled with Hailey.

Her cheek throbbed with pain, but she nodded. "We're fine," she whispered.

"Come on. We need to get out of here," Nate said grimly.

She shifted Hailey in her arms and made her way toward Nate. He put his hand on the small of her back, guiding her back toward the motel. He paused just long enough to pick up the suitcase she'd dropped and brought it along with them.

She didn't want to go anywhere near the man who'd hit her, but forced herself to trust Nate. They passed the black car, and she couldn't help glancing over in that direction.

All she could see was the vehicle listing to one side. It took a minute for her to realize the driver's side tires were flat.

Had Nate done that to prevent the man from following them? And where was the driver?

She shivered, her stomach clenching with dread. She hadn't heard the sound of gunfire, but she had to believe Nate had neutralized him somehow. She was deeply thankful he'd noticed she was gone and had come after her.

But how had the driver of the black car found her in the first place?

They must have known she was with Nate. What had he said back at the mall? He'd called for backup? Anyone with a scanner could have heard that information.

Including the dirty cop who'd tried to frame her as a drug addict.

Nate opened the back passenger door of his car and she quickly put Hailey into her booster seat. When Melissa was about to crawl in beside her daughter, Nate stopped her with a firm hand on her arm.

"In front, with me."

She swallowed hard and nodded, shutting the door and then climbing into the passenger seat. Nate slid in behind the wheel, and soon they were back on the road, heading west, leaving the lights of the city behind.

Silence hung heavy between them.

"What happened to the driver?" she finally asked.

"He's unconscious, but he'll be fine," Nate said in a cold, clipped tone. "Do you mind telling me what you were thinking when you left like that in the middle of the night?"

*Protecting you*, she thought, but she held her tongue.

"What? No snappy comeback? Do you realize how cold it is outside? What about your daughter?" He was starting to raise his volume, and Hailey whimpered, making him lower his voice. "Where were you going to go without a car?"

She swallowed hard. "I planned to call for a taxi."

"And go where?" he pressed.

"The bus station." She looked away from him, staring out at the darkness through the passenger-side window. Several houses were decorated with brightly colored Christmas lights, reminding her of home.

Not her apartment in South Carolina, but the home where she'd grown up. Where she'd lived with her father. Gone to school. Dated Nate. She closed her eyes and pressed her forehead against the cool glass. She'd been so happy back then. How had everything gone so wrong?

"I shouldn't be surprised you tried to leave without telling me. After all, that's your usual response."

The bitter note to his voice made her feel terrible. She forced herself to turn and look at him. "I'm sorry, Nate. I'm sorry I hurt you all those years ago, and I'm sorry I hurt you now. Obviously I've put you in danger, too.

They must know you're with me. Otherwise they never would have found us."

"Yeah, and frankly that's what's bothering me the most," Nate said. "Maybe you should try being honest with me for once. Before we all end up dead."

She sucked in a harsh breath as the reality of what he was saying struck home. He was absolutely right. Her attempt to protect him had backfired in a big way.

If there had been two men instead of one, this situation could have ended much differently.

They all might have been killed. Murdered in cold blood.

"You know the identity of the five men you saw that night, don't you?" Nate asked.

"Not all of them, but yes, I knew one of them besides the cop," she admitted.

"Who?"

She licked her dry lips. "A man with an important job."

"Yeah? Like what?"

She forced the words past her constricted throat. "Like the mayor of Brookmont, Tom McAllister."

"Uncle Tom?" Nate repeated hoarsely. "My uncle Tom?"

"Yes. I'm sorry, Nate." Melissa knew she should have felt better now that the secret was out, but she didn't.

Because she wasn't at all sure Nate would believe her. Why would he take her side over his uncle's? This was exactly the reason she'd left without saying anything to him all those years ago.

She shivered again with fear that chilled her to the bone. These were men who'd tried to discredit her as a drug addict. When that hadn't worked, they'd set out to kill her. If Nate decided to haul her in to be questioned, there was no telling what might happen. They'd lied before, why not try to frame her again?

Or worse, set up some sort of scheme to have her killed in jail?

A sense of desperate hopelessness pierced her heart. She absolutely needed to find a way to make Nate believe her.

Or risk losing Hailey, forever.

# FOUR

Nate didn't want to believe Melissa's claim. Ridiculous to think his uncle Tom was part of some big cover-up. Especially something as serious as murder. Tom McAllister was the mayor of Brookmont. Why on earth would he get involved in something criminal?

But there was no denying Melissa was in trouble. He'd been livid when he'd seen the guy slap her across the face. It was clear the guy's intent was to take Melissa with him, and there was no telling what might have happened if Nate hadn't got there in time. Thank goodness he'd heard her door shutting behind her when she'd left the motel. It had taken him a few minutes to verify that she was gone.

A few minutes that could have cost her life.

But was it really possible that his uncle Tom was involved?

Nate shook his head helplessly. He tightened his grip on the steering wheel and considered his options. Taking Melissa and Hailey straight to his boss was top on his list. Griff was a good, honest cop, and Nate could trust his boss to get to the bottom of whatever was going on.

Or he could take Melissa somewhere safe and begin investigating this on his own.

As much as he'd rather do the latter, he knew that it was a better option to take her to his boss. But it was one o'clock in the morning. There wouldn't be anyone at the sheriff's department headquarters other than the single dispatcher who manned the graveyard shift.

He reached for his phone and handed it over to Melissa. "Do me a favor and take the battery out of the back so I can't be traced. And you need to ditch your phone, too."

She grimaced but did as he asked, dropping both the device and the battery back into the cup holders located in the center console. Then she opened her window and tossed the disposable phone she'd been using.

"Nate, please, you have to believe me," Melissa said in a low, desperate tone, as if reading his turbulent thoughts. "You asked me why I didn't come to you after I witnessed the murder. Well, this is the reason. I was afraid your uncle would turn you against me."

He clenched his jaw so tight his temple ached. "Why would my uncle be involved in covering up a murder?"

"I don't know," Melissa insisted, frustration edging her voice. "I wish I had answers for you, but I don't."

"Yeah, and isn't that convenient?" He felt his anger rising and did his best to lower his tone so he wouldn't disturb Hailey. "You've been keeping secrets from me since I saw you on the escalator. Give me one good reason why I should believe you now."

"Because unfortunately, you were right," she whispered. "Now that you've helped me, I'm afraid you're in as much danger as I am."

"Maybe, but I think it's time I listen to my instincts, which are telling me to hand you over to my boss right now."

Her eyes widened with fear. "If you do that, they'll

find a way to kill me." The grim certainty in her tone nagged at him. "Tell me one thing, Nate. How did they find us at that hotel? You said yourself it's a cop-friendly place. How many cops would know to look for your vehicle there?"

Good question—one that had bothered him from the moment the guy in the black car had grabbed and hit Melissa. It couldn't be a coincidence that they'd been found so quickly. "I don't know," he admitted.

"Please don't take me in. Not when there are dirty policemen involved who obviously won't stop until I'm dead."

He couldn't deny the fact that she was in danger. And if corrupt cops were in on this, keeping her safe would be even more difficult. He let out a heavy sigh and continued driving through the night.

Melissa was right. He couldn't take her in. Not yet.

Not until he knew what they were dealing with.

"Okay, fine," he agreed in a resigned tone. "But no more lies, Melissa. No more escape attempts, either. We work together from this point forward. Understand?"

"Yes," she whispered. "I'm sorry I dragged you into this mess. I know this wasn't at all what you bargained for."

"It's not your fault," he said. In all fairness, she hadn't dragged him into anything. He was the one who'd recognized her on the escalator. And he was the one who'd followed her through the mall. Shooting and wounding two men hadn't been part of the initial plan, but he knew that given the same set of circumstances, he'd do it all again without hesitation.

"Maybe not entirely my fault, but I'm concerned that your reputation will suffer if you continue to help me," she said in a resigned tone.

He didn't bother pointing out that his reputation had already taken a hit the moment he'd decided to leave the crime scene at the mall.

The way she truly seemed to care about his fate helped ease his anger and frustration at waking up and discovering she'd sneaked away during the night.

"I can't worry about my reputation," he said, even though being a cop was important to him. "Hopefully I'll be able to salvage it once we get to the bottom of this mess."

"I hope so," she whispered, resting her head back against the seat. "I truly hope so."

Nate reached over to give her hand a reassuring squeeze, a bit surprised when she responded by tightening her fingers around his and flashing a tentative smile.

They would uncover the truth of the murder Melissa had witnessed twelve years ago.

Because the alternative was too painful to contemplate.

Melissa stared down at their joined hands for a long moment, humbled by Nate's forgiveness. He had every right to be angry, but at least he wasn't taking her to his boss.

She was sorry that she'd inadvertently involved Nate, but she was relieved that she and Hailey weren't alone. If Nate truly believed her, then maybe they could get to the bottom of this by working together.

The warmth of the car caused her eyelids to droop heavily, but she forced them open. She was going to be Nate's partner in this, and she needed to stay awake and alert.

Glancing into the backseat, she was glad to see Hailey had fallen asleep.

"Where are we going?" she asked when Nate turned onto a remote country road.

"Another motel. We need somewhere to crash for what's left of the night," he said. "But I'm not about to use anyplace I've been before."

She was relieved to hear that, although that meant they might be forced to use a credit card.

She racked her brain for an alternate plan but couldn't come up with anything better. "I'd offer my father's house, but I'm sure they have the place staked out, since they found me at the hospital."

"Yeah, I was thinking of using one of my buddies' places," he admitted. "But if they know who I am, it won't be too hard to find out the names of my friends, and I don't want to expose any of them or their families to danger."

She didn't blame him. She thought about the church friends she'd left back in South Carolina and knew she wouldn't be willing to put any of them in harm's way, either.

"There's a place up ahead," Nate said, breaking into her thoughts. "It's small and well off the highway. Should work for our needs."

"Sounds good." She hoped and prayed his uniform would convince the motel clerk to let them pay cash rather than leaving an electronic trail.

Nate pulled into a parking space near the lobby, then turned to face her. "It will be easier to request one room, pretending we're a family. I'll make sure there are two double beds. You and Hailey can share one, and I'll crash on the other."

"All right," she agreed.

Nate slid out from behind the wheel and then disappeared inside. He returned about fifteen minutes later, a satisfied expression on his face.

"I convinced the clerk to take cash, so we should be safe for now."

"Great," she murmured. "I'm exhausted. And sore."

"You need some ice for your face," Nate added with a frown.

She was touched by his concern, although a bruise was the least of her concerns. She was just glad they'd escaped anything worse.

He drove up to the door of their room, pulling the suitcase he'd rescued out of the backseat. "We're in room 5," he told her.

She unbuckled Hailey from the booster seat and carried her daughter inside. It took her a few minutes to get Hailey out of her winter clothes, but thankfully the little girl didn't put up a fight. Soon she had her tucked into the bed closest to the wall.

She turned to face Nate and frowned when she noticed he'd brought in Hailey's child safety seat. "It's probably better to keep that in the backseat in case we have to leave in a hurry."

"I'm planning to find someplace to stash my car," he said. "You and Hailey get some sleep. Don't wait up for me. I don't know how long I'll be gone."

After everything she'd been through, she wasn't looking forward to staying in the tiny motel room alone. But of course, hiking through the snow carrying her daughter wasn't an option, either. "Try not to go too far," she said.

"I won't," Nate promised. The smile that tugged at his mouth reminded her of the way he had looked as a hunky teenager. Too handsome for his own good.

As he let himself out the door, back into the cold winter night, she crossed over to the window, moving the heavy curtain enough to watch him drive away.

Biting back the urge to rush outside and beg him to stay.

Nate drove around the area, looking for a place to hide his vehicle. The trees were bare of leaves, and anything dark showed up all too easily against the snow-covered ground. Too bad he didn't have a white car.

After a couple of miles, he found an abandoned farmhouse, complete with a barn that unfortunately looked as if a strong wind would cause it to come tumbling down.

Since it was better than anything else he'd passed, he drove up through the snow to the crooked doors. He got out of the car and pulled them open, then drove inside.

After locking up his vehicle, he closed the barn doors and then broke off a branch from an evergreen tree and used it to obliterate his tire tracks and footprints. Maybe he was being paranoid, but better safe than sorry.

By the time he reached the road, he was sweating beneath his winter jacket. The result of his attempt to hide the location of his car wasn't perfect, but it should work.

Especially since he was absolutely positive he hadn't been followed. The road was isolated and empty, which suited him just fine.

Shrugging out of his jacket, he tied it securely around his waist so he could jog the mile back to the motel. Thankfully it was late enough that he could use the center of the highway, where there wasn't any snow or ice.

Running through the night gave him a strange sense of peace. As he ran he tried to formulate their next steps. Get some rest, obviously, but after that, they needed to figure out where to start their investigation.

He considered confronting his uncle but didn't want

to do that without some kind of proof. Something other than Melissa's word. Not because he didn't believe her, but because he did.

No, the proof they needed was something indisputable. Something that couldn't be discredited as a lie from an unreliable source. Eyewitness testimony was good, but twelve years had passed since the original crime had been committed. They needed to prove that Melissa witnessed a murder.

Which meant they needed the identity of the man who'd died that night.

Nate knew his way around computers and technology, although he didn't have anything with him. First thing in the morning, they needed to find a laptop so he could get decent access to the internet. Having his personal laptop would be even better so that he could use his work search engines.

Satisfied that he had some semblance of a plan, he increased his pace until he could see the lights of the motel. As he came closer, he slowed his pace in an effort to cool down.

He quietly let himself inside the room, hoping not to disturb Hailey or Melissa.

But the moment he crossed the threshold, Melissa raised her head and glanced over at him.

"Sorry to wake you," he whispered, closing the door softly behind him.

"You didn't," she assured him. "I couldn't sleep."

"Get some rest," he advised. "We have work to do in the morning."

It wasn't easy to see in the darkness, but he thought she nodded. "Good night, Nate."

"Good night." He made his way to the bathroom so he could take a shower. Nothing he could do to salvage his uniform, which was damp with sweat. By the time he emerged twenty minutes later, he could hear Melissa's deep, even breaths.

She was asleep at last. He crawled into the empty bed and did his best to shut down his brain.

It seemed like barely an hour later when he woke up to Hailey's plaintive whining. "Mommy, I'm hungry."

"Shh, we have to be quiet and wait until Mr. Nate wakes up, okay? Look, I found a kids' movie for you."

Nate pried his eyelids open, trying to read the time on his watch. Five minutes past six in the morning. He swallowed a groan. It wasn't the first time he'd been forced to work on less than four hours of sleep.

Man, he was getting too old for this.

"I'm awake," he managed, propping himself up on one elbow. "Give me a few minutes and I'll run back and get the car."

"The motel offers a free continental breakfast," Melissa informed him. "I'll take Hailey over there while you rest for a few more hours."

He pushed himself upright and scrubbed his hands over his face, wishing for a razor. "You were up as late as I was," he said. "Just give me a few minutes to get ready and we'll all go to breakfast together."

"Okay," she agreed.

He headed into the bathroom to wash up and use the facilities. Just as he opened the bathroom door, he heard Melissa talking.

He frowned, realizing she must be on the motel phone, since she'd tossed hers out the window.

He strode into the room to find her sitting on the end of the bed, holding the receiver to her ear. "When did he die?" she asked.

He realized that she must be talking with the hospital. He crossed over and sat down beside her.

"Okay, thanks for letting me know," she said. She disconnected from the call and glanced up at him, her eyes filling with tears.

"I just wanted to check on my dad's condition. He passed away about an hour ago," she said in a low voice.

"I'm so sorry for your loss," he said, wrapping his arm around her slim shoulders.

She nodded and buried her face in her hands, her shoulders shaking with suppressed sobs.

He gathered her into his arms, feeling helpless to do anything but hold her in an attempt to offer comfort. Nate knew that even though Melissa and her father hadn't seen each other in person for the past twelve years, they'd remained close. After all, she'd mentioned that her father's dying wish was to see his granddaughter.

"He was a good man," she whispered.

"I know," he agreed.

Melissa surprised him by wrapping her arms around his waist and pressing her face into the hollow of his shoulder. Thankfully Hailey seemed to be preoccupied with her television show, despite her earlier complaints about being hungry.

Nate ran his hand down Melissa's back, trying to think of something to say. "Is there anything I can do to help? What about funeral arrangements?"

He felt her draw in a deep breath and then let it out slowly. She lifted her head. "Thanks, but he's already taken care of everything. I'm just upset at knowing that I won't be able to attend his funeral."

He brushed her damp hair away from her cheeks. "We

could try to find a way," he offered, even though he had no idea how they'd manage that.

She sniffled loudly and swiped at her tears. "It's too dangerous for Hailey," she said. "I can't risk putting her at risk, not when I've already had a chance to say goodbye."

Nate had to tamp down a flash of anger. It wasn't fair that Melissa had to forgo her father's funeral.

"We can try to sneak in before the funeral home is open to the public," he offered.

"No, that's not necessary," she murmured. "In my heart, I know that my father is in a much better place with God. That will be enough to see me through the next few days."

He was touched by her faith and couldn't think of anything to say in reply. She stared up at him with her wide hazel eyes, and for a moment it seemed as if time had stood still. The old feelings he'd buried long ago came rushing to the surface.

Reacting instinctively, he bent his head intending to capture her mouth in a poignant kiss.

# FIVE

Melissa froze for a split second before melting against Nate, and responding to his kiss. The twelve year gap in their relationship faded away, and it was as if they were young and in love once again, excited about the future possibilities stretching ahead of them.

And if she was honest with herself, she'd admit Nate's kiss filled a tiny void in her heart that she'd done her best to ignore ever since.

"Mommy? Why are you kissing Mr. Nate?"

Hailey's voice jerked her roughly back to the present, and she quickly pulled away from Nate, her cheeks flaming with embarrassment. She jumped up from the foot of the bed and gave herself a mental shake.

What on earth had she been thinking? She couldn't allow herself to forget about Hailey. She was the most important person in her life.

Her future didn't include Nate. They were different people now. Her life was about providing a safe and secure future for her daughter, not rekindling an old high school romance.

"Um, well, I guess I was just sad for a minute, Hailey. But now it's time for breakfast. Isn't that right, Nate?" she said, forcing a smile on her face.

"Sure," Nate responded in a low, gravelly tone. She reached for Hailey's coat, avoiding his gaze, because she didn't want to know if he had been as affected by their kiss as she'd been.

When she managed to get Hailey's winter gear on, she glanced around for her coat, only to realize belatedly that Nate was holding it out for her.

She swallowed hard and slipped her arms into the sleeves, murmuring her thanks as he pulled her parka up over her shoulders. Her pulse beat frantically in her chest, and she couldn't remember the last time a man had knocked her off balance like this.

As much as she'd loved Jeremy, they'd been friends long before they'd married. They'd met at her church group and having finally felt safe, she'd allowed herself to date him. But even then, there hadn't been this strange frisson of adrenaline that raced through her bloodstream at his slightest touch. Jeremy had been sweet, kind and gentle. Everything she'd wanted in a husband. In a father for her children.

So why was she suddenly acutely aware of Nate?

Stress. She was under an incredible amount of stress. Not just because of her father's death, but in the daunting task of attempting to figure out who'd murdered the man she'd seen get stabbed, while trying to stay alive and out of harm's way.

With her feet back on steady ground, Melissa took Hailey's hand as they walked outside into the frigid air. The sunny sky was an extreme contrast to the wind chill. She shivered and quickened her pace in an effort to reach the lobby faster.

"Brr, it's cold, Mommy," Hailey said, echoing her thoughts.

"I know, sweetie. But look at all the snow. Isn't it

pretty?" She forced herself to sound happy, even though her heart mourned the passing of her dad.

Hailey nodded eagerly. "Very pretty."

Nate stepped ahead and opened the door for them. Melissa ushered Hailey inside in front of her, grateful for the warmth.

There was a pair of truckers inside the lobby enjoying breakfast, and instantly Hailey cringed and clung to her hand.

"No!" Hailey cried.

"Shh, it's okay, sweetie. You don't have to be afraid of all strangers," she hastened to reassure her daughter. Apparently all the discussions at the preschool about staying away from strangers, along with their mad dash through the mall, had really frightened her daughter. "We're okay here with Mr. Nate. Remember how he's been keeping us safe? There's no need to be afraid."

Hailey didn't respond, her gaze full of doubt, and she stuck to Melissa like a burr as they approached the breakfast bar.

"What would you like to eat, Hailey?" Nate asked in a cheerful tone. "Cereal? Toast?"

Melissa hated seeing her daughter so afraid, although she shouldn't have been caught off guard by Hailey's response to the strangers. After all Hailey had been through since they arrived in Milwaukee, she was surprised the little girl was coping as well as she was.

"Look, they have your favorite fruity cereal," she said, injecting enthusiasm into her tone. "How about that?"

"Okay," she said in a quiet, subdued voice.

"We can sit at this table here," Nate said, choosing the table farthest from the door and from the two truckers, who hadn't paid them any attention.

"Great. Hailey, why don't you sit with Mr. Nate while I get you some breakfast?" she suggested as they made their way over to where Nate stood. "Do you want anything besides cereal?"

"I want toast, too, with strawberry jelly." Hailey nodded her head for emphasis. Melissa was relieved to see that the stark moment of fear had faded from her daughter's eyes.

"All right. Just wait here and I'll be right back." Melissa went to the buffet counter to get Hailey's breakfast, ignoring the way her stomach rumbled with hunger at the rich scent of freshly brewed coffee.

She returned to the table, only to stop short when she caught a glimpse of Nate's and Hailey's heads bent close as they worked on coloring a picture together. Her chest tightened, making it difficult to breathe. For a moment she wished for something she couldn't have, but then she shook off the useless emotion with an effort.

Hailey was Jeremy's daughter, not Nate's. And she'd loved her husband. Nate was just being nice. Enough with confusing the past with the present. They had work to do.

"Here you go," she said loudly as she approached the table.

"Goody," Hailey said, quickly abandoning her picture and turning her attention to her food.

Melissa pulled out a chair to sit down, but Nate stopped her with a hand on her arm. "Why don't you get yourself something, too?" he suggested. "I'll stay here with Hailey."

Had Nate always been so gallant? So considerate? She couldn't help thinking that he'd grown up to be quite an amazing guy.

"All right." She returned to the buffet, not just because she was hungry but also because she needed a bit of distance from Nate.

She was grateful for his determination to protect her and Hailey, but remaining in proximity and working with him would be more difficult than she'd anticipated. At least, on a personal level.

Grimly she realized she'd need every ounce of strength and willpower she possessed to get through the next few days.

Because allowing herself to become emotionally involved with Nate again was not part of her plan.

Nate couldn't seem to tear his gaze from Melissa as she filled a mug of coffee and helped herself to a toasted English muffin.

Not just because she was beautiful. There was something about her that tugged at his senses.

He scrubbed his hands over his face, willing the feelings away. Obviously he shouldn't have kissed her—still had no idea why he had. He'd only intended to offer comfort, but that plan had backfired in a big way.

Watching Hailey as she dug into her fruity cereal only reminded him that there was no going back to the past. Melissa was vulnerable. She'd just lost her father and her life was in danger. Plus he suspected she still had feelings for her dead husband, and even if she was willing to consider getting involved in another relationship, it was clear that she'd made a life for herself and Hailey down in South Carolina.

Now that her father had passed away, there would be nothing to keep her here once they figured out who'd murdered a man and why.

Still, Hailey was a cutie, and for a moment he found himself wanting what so many of his fellow teammates had. A wife and family to come home to. Not that he knew much about growing up in a happy household.

"Your turn," Melissa said as she returned to sit beside Hailey.

He nodded and rose to his feet. What he desperately needed was a megadose of caffeine to wipe away the cobwebs from his brain. A clear head to figure out their next steps.

For one thing, he had to jog back to the old barn where he'd hidden his car. From there, he needed to get his hands on a computer. Maybe he could risk going to his place to pick up his state-of-the-art laptop.

Alone, he wouldn't think twice about doing what needed to be done, but he had Melissa and Hailey to consider. No way would he expose them to danger.

"I'll be back in about twenty minutes or so," he said once he'd finished his breakfast and gulped two cups of coffee. "I should get here before checkout time."

"All right," Melissa agreed. "I'll keep Hailey occupied with the kids' channel while we wait."

He nodded but then hesitated, turning back to face her. "Now, remember, you gave me your word, Melissa," he warned in a low voice. "Don't go off on your own."

She lifted her chin and met his gaze square-on. "I don't break my promises," she assured him. "I know I took off before, but we will be here when you return."

It was on the tip of his tongue to refresh her memory on what had happened when she'd run away the night before, but he managed to bite back the scathing comment. There was nothing they could do but move forward from here.

Nate walked outside in time to see the two truck drivers heading to their respective rigs. "Either of you heading south?" he asked. "I could use a lift to the next intersection, just a few miles up the road."

Maybe it was his uniform, because the two men looked at each other and shrugged. "Yeah, I'm heading that way," the shorter of the two said. "Hop in."

"Thanks. I really appreciate your help."

The trucker didn't say much, and Nate didn't either. The mile he'd jogged last night seemed like nothing while riding in the truck. "Here you go," the guy said, pulling up to a stop sign.

"Thanks again," Nate said before jumping down. He waited until the driver pulled away and was out of sight before he walked back to the old barn.

The area around the outside of the structure didn't look as if it had been disturbed since he'd left last night. Maybe he'd been foolish to go to such extreme measures.

He hauled open the barn doors and quickly backed his car onto the driveway. He climbed out to close the doors behind him and then made a left turn toward the motel.

He made it back so quickly, he could see that Melissa and Hailey were still sitting inside the restaurant. Nate parked his vehicle outside their room and then replaced the battery in his phone. He took a deep breath and called Jenna Reed, the only female cop on their SWAT team.

She answered on the second ring. "Nate? Where are you?"

"I—uh—need a favor."

"Griff is looking for your head to be served up on a platter after the stunt you pulled at the mall."

He winced at Jenna's bluntness. "Yeah, well, things are complicated. A woman and her five-year-old child are in danger, so I took them someplace safe."

"Listen, Nate, you seriously have to call Griff as soon as possible."

"I will, but I'm calling you because I need help."

Jenna didn't speak for a long moment. And honestly, he couldn't blame her. Helping him would only put her on Griff's bad side.

"Never mind," he said hastily. "I don't want to drag you down with me."

"What do you need?" Jenna asked. "I don't have a lot of time. We're shorthanded with you AWOL and Simms handing in his resignation."

"Simms resigned?" he echoed in surprise. "What's that about?"

"No clue," Jenna said shortly. "But you're burning daylight, Freemont. Tell me what you need and I'll be happy to help."

As much as he hated involving anyone else, he figured this favor wouldn't put Jenna in too much danger. "Okay, here's the deal. I need my computer, and I have reason to believe that someone might be watching my house. I was hoping you could slip in, grab it for me and slip out without anyone noticing. Once I have computer access, I should be fine working this thing alone."

"Piece of cake," Jenna said, obviously willing to assist in any way possible. "I should have time to get your computer as long as we don't get a SWAT call."

"Great. If you could meet me someplace, I'd appreciate it. Maybe out at the strip mall on Highway 24?"

"Sure thing. Anything else you need as long as I'm going to your place?"

The thought of Jenna going through his closet to pick out clothes didn't sit well with him. He'd be better off buying new items. "No, but thanks. I'll buy what I need at the mall."

"I'll bring some cash, too," Jenna said. "That way you'll avoid leaving an electronic trail."

Taking money from Jenna wasn't much better, but then again, he was good for the loan. "Okay, thanks again. I really appreciate your help."

"No problem," Jenna responded lightly. Despite the fact that they'd worked together for over a year, she kept her distance from the rest of the team when it came to anything outside of work-related concerns. Nate suspected she did that on purpose to avoid appearing weak. Or to avoid getting too personally involved with anyone she worked with. Either way, he totally understood her logic. "I'll be in touch later."

He disconnected from the call, then removed his battery from the phone once again. No reason to stop being paranoid now. He slid out of the driver's seat in time to see Melissa and Hailey making their way back to their motel room.

"You're back already?" Melissa asked.

"One of the truckers gave me a lift," he acknowledged, reaching over to unlock the motel door for her.

"Okay, I'll pack our things so we can leave," she murmured.

"No rush. We may as well wait until checkout time." He didn't want to get to the meet point too early. And it wouldn't take more than fifteen minutes to pick up some jeans and a sweatshirt to have something to wear other than his uniform.

He glanced at his watch, trying to estimate how much time Jenna would need to sneak in and out of his house with his computer. Difficult to know, since she'd have to figure out if anyone was watching the place or not.

Nate let out a heavy sigh. Allowing someone else to do something potentially dangerous on his behalf wasn't easy. Not that he didn't trust Jenna's skills, but sitting here and waiting while others exposed themselves to danger didn't sit well with him.

And he felt even more guilty knowing that Aaron Simms had resigned. Staffing was always dicey around the holidays, anyway, but with Simms gone, things would be tighter than usual.

He needed to find some evidence of the murder Melissa had witnessed, the sooner the better. Once he had some leads to go on, he might be able to approach Griff for help and support.

And hey, maybe Griff would be less likely to fire him now that Simms had resigned.

Melissa's tentative voice interrupted his thoughts. "We're ready to leave whenever you are."

"Okay. Did you grab the toiletries from the bathroom, too?" he asked. "There's no sense in leaving them behind."

"I tossed them in our suitcase," Melissa said.

He nodded and crossed over to pick up the bag. Its light weight only reminded him that they hadn't planned on staying here in Milwaukee for very long.

He stored the luggage in the trunk of his car while Melissa tucked Hailey into her booster seat. Once they were all settled in, he drove back out onto the highway.

"I'm planning to stop at a mall that's about twenty minutes from here," he told her. "Might be a good time to pick up anything else you and Hailey need."

Melissa's smile was a bit strained. "We're okay. I can't think of anything in particular."

Nate found himself wondering about Melissa's life down in South Carolina. He didn't know what she or her husband had done for work or who her friends were. He was bothered by the fact that she'd been willing to give up her life in Wisconsin to start over using a new name. Although she'd said herself that she didn't feel as if she'd had a choice.

They rode in silence for a good ten minutes before Melissa reached out to put her hand on his arm. "Nate? Do you think it's possible that dark green van is following us?"

He frowned, checking in his rearview mirror. The van wasn't hugging his bumper but seemed to be keeping pace. He tried speeding up and then slowing down, and still it stayed about two car lengths behind.

Nate wished he'd taken the interstate. This particular stretch of highway was fairly deserted. He scanned the area, trying to think of a good way to lose the possible tail.

"Hang on," he warned as he put on his left turn signal. He slowed to a stop but then gunned the engine, making a hard right at the last minute.

The other vehicle swerved sharply but recovered quickly, and this time, it was clear the driver was following them. Nate pushed the speed limit, aware that he couldn't afford to take too many chances with Melissa and Hailey in the car.

"Should I call for help?" Melissa asked, her voice trembling with fear. "Where's your phone?"

He had to admire her courage, considering she was just as afraid of the police as she was of the driver behind them. He dug out his cell. "Yes, here—call 911. We're in Washington County, so we should be able to trust them."

Melissa dialed the emergency number, and he could hear the ringing on the other end of the phone as she waited for the dispatcher to answer.

Abruptly the van came up alongside him, driving in the wrong lane on the highway. Nate glanced over and then gaped in shock as the guy in the passenger seat lowered his window and aimed a gun at him.

"Look out!" he shouted, hitting the brakes hard enough that the car shot past them, even as he heard the sound of a bullet hitting the side of his car.

"I dropped your phone!" Melissa cried.

"Mommy!" Hailey screamed.

Nate wrestled with the steering wheel, trying to keep them from crashing. He managed to yank it to the side enough to make an illegal U-turn. When he was facing the opposite direction, he punched the gas, anxious to get as far away as possible.

"I think they're still behind us!" Melissa whispered hoarsely as she frantically searched for the phone she'd dropped.

Nate gripped the steering wheel tightly, his foot to the floor, as Melissa finally connected with the 911 operator. She gave their approximate location, and the dispatcher promised to send help to the scene.

But as Nate watched the green van gaining on them in the rearview mirror, he was afraid the police response would arrive too late.

# SIX

Clenching her teeth together, Melissa tried to remain calm, despite the overwhelming sense of dread. She wanted to crawl into the backseat and throw her body over Hailey's. But the seat belts had locked up tight when the car braked, and Nate was now driving like a maniac in his effort to stay ahead of the van.

She whispered, "Please, Lord, keep us safe in Your care. Guide us away from the threat behind us. We place our lives in Your hands. Amen."

"Sing 'Jesus Loves Me,' Mommy," Hailey begged.

She sang the church lullaby while Nate continued to speed down the country highway. From what she could tell, the other vehicle seemed to be gradually closing in on them.

When Hailey joined in singing, tears pricked Melissa's eyes, and her heart squeezed in her chest. She knew God had a master plan, but she sincerely hoped that He would spare her daughter's life.

The high-pitched scream of a siren pierced the air. Melissa faltered in her singing, glancing wildly for the source of the siren. Would the police get there in time?

There was a loud crack as a bullet penetrated the back

window of the car. Hailey screamed again and Melissa twisted in her seat, trying to figure out if she'd been hit.

"Hailey, are you okay? Where do you hurt? Tell Mommy where you hurt!"

"I'm scared," she cried between heartbreaking sobs.

Melissa couldn't see any blood. The bullet hole was on the opposite side of the glass from where Hailey's booster seat was.

She grabbed Nate's arm. "Are you okay? Did the bullet hit you?"

"I'm fine," he said curtly.

Melissa was relieved and panicked at the same time. "Nate, we have to do something. They're shooting at us!"

"I know, but hear those sirens? We have to hang on long enough for the police to get here."

She knew Nate was right, but listening to Hailey crying was too much to bear. She wrestled with the seat belt, finally managing to get the clasp to release. She hastily scrambled between the front seats to get to Hailey.

"What are you doing?" Nate asked harshly. "You're exposing yourself to more danger."

She ignored him, hovering over her daughter. "Shh, it's okay, we're okay," she said, rubbing her hand over her daughter's hair. She felt along the child's body, making sure that there wasn't any sign of injury. "The police are going to be here any second."

"No bad guys," Hailey sobbed.

"Let's sing, okay? Come on, Hailey. 'Yes, Jesus loves me! The Bible tells me so,'" she sang in a soft tone. Soon Hailey joined in, and together they continued the entire first verse and the chorus.

The sirens grew louder, so Melissa paused and glanced at Nate. "Is the van still behind us?"

"I don't see it anymore. It dropped back as soon as the sirens grew louder. I think we're okay for now."

Melissa dropped her chin to her chest in a wave of relief. "Thank You, Lord," she whispered.

She could feel the car slowing to a stop as Nate pulled over to the side of the road. The sheriff's deputy vehicle came up right alongside them, the lights on the top of the squad car flashing blue and red.

"Is everyone okay in there?" the deputy asked with obvious concern.

"We're fine. They shot through the rear window, but no one was hit," Nate said.

"You're a deputy?" the officer asked in surprise.

"Yeah, Deputy Freemont from the Milwaukee County Sheriff's Department."

"I'm Deputy Holmes. Deputy Shaker is searching for the other vehicle. Did you happen to get a plate number?" Holmes asked.

"No, things happened too fast," Nate admitted. "They shot at me twice. I'm fairly certain there's a bullet hole somewhere in the side of the car."

The deputy glanced into the backseat where she was sitting with Hailey. Melissa froze, fear lodging in the back of her throat. Logically she understood it wasn't likely that this deputy would know the cop involved in the murder she'd witnessed, but her distrust toward the police was deeply ingrained in her blood.

"Ma'am, are you sure you and the child are all right?" he asked.

She did her best to smile. "Yes, we're fine. Thank you." The words came out in a hoarse whisper, but it was the best she could do.

"I'm going to need statements from each of you," Deputy Holmes said. The radio on his collar squawked, and he straightened and turned away, speaking in low tones.

Melissa reached forward to tap Nate's shoulder. He turned in his seat to look at her. "How long is he going to keep us?" she asked. "I don't want him to run a background check on me."

Nate grimaced. "I'm not sure, but I'll see if I can convince him to let us go once we give our statements."

She nodded but couldn't relax. The very real physical threat was over, but that didn't mean she and Hailey were completely in the clear.

Not when there was no way of knowing if her fake ID would stand up to this officer's scrutiny. If it didn't, she couldn't bear to think about the possible consequences.

Nate could feel the tension radiating off Melissa but wasn't sure what he could do to make her feel better. He was grateful he was still in uniform, so the officer who'd come to their rescue easily realized he was one of them.

There was a brotherhood among police officers—at least, most of the time. Nate hoped that this guy would be willing to give him the courtesy of taking him at his word.

Although it was just as likely that the officer would want to conduct a full investigation, which meant doing background checks on both of them. How would Deputy Holmes react if he learned Nate wasn't currently on duty, despite being in uniform? He'd violated a lot of rules in the past twenty-four hours, and being off duty in uniform was just one of them.

Nate didn't want to think about the fact that Griff had so many reasons to fire him.

"I'm afraid my partner lost sight of the van," Deputy Holmes said, breaking into his depressing thoughts.

Nate turned back to face him. "That's not good news," he said. "But maybe we can find the bullet."

"Good point. Let's take a look."

They both searched in the backseat area, estimating by the trajectory the bullet might have taken. When Nate found the bullet lodged in the back of his headrest, he couldn't suppress a shiver.

Way too close.

He pried it out of the wood frame and then handed it to Deputy Holmes.

"Let's go to my squad car so I can take your statements separately," Holmes said.

"No problem." Nate glanced back at Melissa and Hailey. "If you get too cold, start the engine. I won't be long."

Melissa gave a tiny nod, although the pinched expression on her face didn't lessen at all. He knew that she was worried about giving her statement and racked his brain for some way to get Deputy Holmes to expedite the process.

Since Nate had interviewed many people himself, he knew exactly what the deputy wanted to hear. He gave a concise yet thorough account of what happened.

"Is there a reason you were being followed?" Deputy Holmes asked.

Nate didn't want to lie, so he nodded. "Yes, I'm actively involved in a case. Melissa Harris and her daughter Hailey are in danger, and I believe they're the real targets."

Deputy Holmes frowned. "You have a suspect?"

"Not yet, but this is the third attempt I've personally witnessed of someone trying to get to them. I'm meeting one of my colleagues as soon as we're finished here. Together we're going to see if we can come up with a list of suspects." Nate paused and then added, "I'm happy to keep you up to date as our investigation unfolds."

"I'd appreciate that," the deputy said. "You must have some theory of why the woman and her kid are in danger?"

Nate shrugged. "Lots of theories. Nothing I can prove." He hoped Deputy Holmes wouldn't push the issue, because he didn't want to give any additional details. "You know how it is with active investigations."

"Yeah. We'll get the bullet analyzed for you. Why don't you have your lieutenant give mine a call? Our districts can work together to get this guy before he strikes again."

Nate nodded. "Sure. My Lieutenant is Griffin Vaughn."

Deputy Holmes scribbled on the back of a business card and handed it to Nate. "Have him call Lieutenant Max Cooper. I'll give Max a heads-up to expect the call."

"Thanks." Nate slid the card into his breast pocket, hoping Holmes didn't speak to Cooper too soon. "Do you want to interview Melissa Harris now? I'd like to get back on the road soon, to get her and the child stashed in a safe place."

"Understood."

Nate solemnly shook Deputy Holmes's hand. "Thanks again for the quick response. Even though you didn't find the van, at least we're all right."

"Do you need me to escort you to the meeting you've set up with your colleague?" Holmes asked.

Nate considered his options before slowly nodding in agreement. "Actually, that would be great. We're just meeting up at the strip mall off Highway 24."

"No problem."

Nate walked back to his vehicle and slid into the driver's seat. "Your turn," he said, meeting Melissa's gaze in the rearview mirror. "I explained that I'm working a case and that you and Hailey are the real targets."

Her lips thinned, but she nodded and slipped out of the passenger-side door. She hunched her shoulders in her parka as she walked over to the deputy's vehicle.

Nate glanced back at Hailey, hoping to put the child at ease. "Your mom will be right back, okay?"

"Okay," Hailey whispered.

"Why don't you teach me the song you and your mom were singing?" Nate asked. "I've never heard it before."

"You don't know the words to 'Jesus Loves Me'?" Hailey asked, clearly surprised.

"I know the first line," Nate said. He sang it, imitating the lyrics he'd heard coming from the backseat, and then paused, waiting for Hailey to sing the rest. He remembered hearing Melissa praying while he was doing a good imitation of a race car driver.

Oddly enough, listening to her prayer had helped keep him calm and focused. Which was strange, since he hadn't embraced church and faith the way so many of his buddies had.

But maybe he should? After all, it seemed to work for Melissa and Hailey. Could be that he was missing out on something important.

And he liked the idea of Melissa showing him the way.

Melissa twisted her cold white fingers together, hoping Deputy Holmes wouldn't notice. She gave her account of how the green van had followed them and then came up alongside to shoot at Nate.

"So you think Deputy Freemont was the intended target?" Holmes asked.

She swallowed hard. "Yes, for the moment. But I suspect that's because he was driving. I believe the van intended for us to crash."

"Surely you have some idea who's after you?" he asked.

Melissa had no idea how much Nate had told him. "Actually, I don't know. If I did, I would give Deputy Freemont a name and have him arrested."

"What about your daughter's father?" Holmes pressed. "Is he the one after you? Are you in some sort of custody dispute?"

She forced herself to look straight into the deputy's eyes, hoping that he would believe her. "No. My husband, Jeremy Harris, died before Hailey was born."

"I'm sorry for your loss," he said, looking embarrassed.

"Thank you. Is there anything else you need? I'm sorry to say this, but I don't feel safe staying in this area, considering it wasn't that long ago that someone tried to kill us."

"That's all for now."

She nearly buckled with relief, but forced herself to smile and hold out her hand. "Thank you for coming as soon as you did," she murmured. "I'm very grateful."

"You're welcome. I just wish we'd captured the ones responsible."

"Me, too. Have a merry Christmas, Deputy." Melissa pushed open the car door and climbed out of the vehicle, quickly making her way back to Nate. She slid into the passenger seat, grateful that he'd left the motor idling to keep the interior warm.

"Are you okay?" Nate asked as he pulled out onto the highway.

"Yes. It wasn't as bad as I anticipated." She rubbed

her hands together, trying to get the feeling back into her numb fingers.

"I let him know this situation was part of an active investigation," Nate said. "He wants Griff to call his boss so they can work together to find the guys who chased us."

Her stomach knotted with fear. "Are you going to call your boss?" she asked.

"Not until I talk to Jenna."

A spear of jealousy hit her out of nowhere. Nate had said he wasn't married and didn't have a girlfriend, so who was Jenna? She reminded herself that since Nate didn't belong to her, it didn't matter who the other woman was. "Oh, are you planning to call her?"

"Jenna is a friend and I arranged for her to meet us at the strip mall. She's bringing my computer so we can start researching the murder you witnessed."

"I see. Are you sure we can trust her?" As soon as the words left her mouth, she wanted to call them back. Why was she questioning Nate's friendship with this woman? If he didn't trust her, he wouldn't have asked her for help.

"I'm sure. She won't go to Griff unless I tell her it's okay."

Melissa blinked. "You mean, you work with her? Jenna is a deputy on the SWAT team?"

"Yes, she's one of our best sharpshooters." Nate smiled. "I told you I'm not seeing anyone. Jenna is a friend and a colleague, nothing more."

Her cheeks grew warm, and she wished she could roll down her window so the arctic air could cool her off. "Your love life is none of my business, Nate."

He was silent for a moment. "Maybe not, but you should know that I wouldn't have kissed you if I was seeing someone else."

She swallowed a groan. Did he have to remind her about that idiotic kiss? The one she never should have indulged in?

The one she wanted to repeat far more than she should?

Melissa twisted in her seat to look at Hailey. "Are you okay back there?" she asked. "Are you cold?"

"I'm not cold," Hailey said, swinging her feet so that they hit the back of Melissa's seat. "Are we almost there, Mommy?"

"Less than ten minutes," Nate spoke up.

"We haven't been driving that long, Hailey," Melissa reminded her. "And will you please stop kicking my seat?"

"Sorry, Mommy," Hailey said, lowering her legs. "I teached Mr. Nate how to sing 'Jesus Loves Me.' Can we sing it again?"

She was surprised to discover they'd been singing songs while she was busy talking to the deputy. "Did you teach him all three verses?" Melissa asked with a smile.

"No, just the first one. Right, Mr. Nate?"

"That's right," Nate agreed. "But, look, Hailey, there's the strip mall up ahead. Why don't we sing later?"

"What's the matter? Did you forget the words already?" Melissa teased him.

Nate grinned. "No, but I doubt I have the best singing voice compared with how amazing you and Hailey sound together."

She was touched by his compliment, which was ridiculous, since he'd only heard them singing in the heat of danger. Melissa shifted in her seat to better pay attention as Nate pulled up next to a rusty and dented sedan. He waved, indicating the deputy who'd followed them could leave now.

"That's Jenna's car?" she asked with a frown. Truthfully, she didn't think it would last very long.

"Her old one. She recently bought a brand-new truck." He rolled down his window as Jenna approached. "I didn't realize you were still driving that thing," he said by way of greeting.

"Actually, I figured we'd swap," Jenna said, bending over to lean her forearms on the edge of the open window. The female cop gave Melissa a curious look. "Hi, I'm Deputy Jenna Reed."

"Melissa Harris, and my daughter, Hailey," she replied. The young, willowy blonde wasn't anything like Melissa expected. She looked tough yet fragile at the same time.

"Thanks for bringing the computer," Nate said. "Did you run into any trouble at my place?"

Jenna hesitated and shrugged. "I managed to get in and out without anyone seeing me, but there was definitely someone staking it out. I wrote down the license plate number and tucked it into your computer case along with some cash."

"Thanks, although I'm surprised you didn't run the plates yourself," Nate said with a grin.

"I will when I get home. I didn't want to be late." Jenna held out her car keys. "But as soon as I realized your house was being watched, I decided to bring my old car with me."

"Thanks, but I hate the thought of putting you in danger," Nate said with a scowl. "We were ambushed while driving here. Luckily no one was injured, but the bullets easily could have hit any of us."

Melissa knew that if Hailey had been on the other side of the car, her daughter would have been hit.

Possibly killed. She shivered and tried not to think about it.

Jenna grimaced. "You were lucky, that's for sure. But I'll be fine. I'll drive your car to our headquarters and leave it there."

Melissa could tell Nate wasn't convinced.

"What's the matter, Freemont?" Jenna demanded. "Haven't you figured out by now I can take care of myself? Admit it. You'd swap in an instant if I was Declan or Isaac."

"Okay, fine, we'll swap rides." Nate pushed open his door, and they quickly exchanged car keys.

It didn't take long to get Hailey's booster seat and Melissa's small suitcase moved over to Jenna's old sedan.

"I threw a duffel of your clothing in there, too, Nate, so no need to shop," Jenna said. "Oh, and here. Bought a couple of disposable phones for you."

Nate took the phones, obviously grateful. "You've thought of everything, haven't you? Thanks."

Jenna shrugged off his gratitude. "Where are you headed?"

"An old fishing cabin. Belongs to the brother of my dad's new wife. I'll give you a call once we get there."

"All right. Stay safe." Jenna lifted her hand and slid into the driver's seat of Nate's dinged-up car.

Surprisingly, Melissa was sad to see the female deputy leave. Was she doing the right thing by going along with Nate? He'd already risked his life multiple times.

And she knew she'd never be able to forgive herself if something terrible happened to him. They had to find out who was behind these recent attempts.

There had been too many close calls already.

# SEVEN

With a frown, Nate tried to remember the directions to Amelia's brother's cabin. He'd been there only once and didn't have an address to punch into a GPS device. He knew the name of the town, though. New Haven. And the cabin was on Lake Haven.

Should he call his father to get the address? At the very least, he should warn his dad to be careful now that he was involved.

The idea of his father being in danger continued to nag at him as he drove. But Melissa's father had never been targeted, so he wanted to believe the same would hold true for his dad. If anything, he'd be watched to see if Nate came home.

"I'm thirsty," Hailey complained.

Nate shot a guilty glance at the clock. The hour was well past noon. "Sorry. I should have thought of stopping earlier," he said to Melissa. "Keep an eye out for something Hailey would like."

"Any fast-food place is fine," she assured him. "Take the next exit."

Nate did as she asked. When he was about to enter the drive-through lane, Melissa put her hand on his arm. "Might be best to go inside so Hailey can use the bathroom."

He nodded, realizing he didn't know much about what kids needed. "Sorry," he mumbled, swinging Jenna's rust bucket into a parking space.

"It's okay," Melissa said. "It would be good to stretch our legs for a bit, too."

He opened the door to the restaurant and then followed them in. While Melissa took Hailey to the restroom, he quickly called his dad using his personal cell phone, since the disposable ones Jenna had given him weren't charged up and ready to go.

"Hi, Nate, you caught me on my way out. How are you?" His father's cheerful tone made him smile. Ever since his dad had met Amelia, he'd been like a new person.

"Good, Dad. How are things at home? Notice anything out of the ordinary?"

"No, why?" His father's tone immediately turned serious. He was a firefighter, which was just as dangerous as being a cop, and he understood all too well the types of situations Nate faced on a daily basis.

"I'm working a case and discovered that someone is watching my house. I don't want to alarm you, but you and Amelia really need to be on alert. If you notice anything out of the ordinary, I want you to call it in. In fact, it might be a good time for you two to take a vacation."

"Six days before Christmas? No way. Amelia will never agree to that. Don't worry, son. We'll be fine."

Nate closed his eyes for a moment, tightening his grip on his phone. "Please be careful, Dad," he said again. "They've already taken shots at me twice now."

"Twice?" his dad echoed in horror. "Where's your boss? Why aren't you in protective custody?"

Nate winced, realizing too late that he shouldn't have mentioned that fact. "I'm fine, Dad. Trust me. Just be on the lookout for any problems, okay? I'll check in on you as often as I can."

"All right," his dad reluctantly agreed. "But I hope you're able to wind this case up before Christmas. We're looking forward to spending some time with you."

"I hope so, too. Take care, Dad." Nate let out a heavy sigh as he disconnected from the call.

"Something wrong?" Melissa asked as she and Hailey approached.

"Not at all," he said, forcing a smile. "What do you want to eat?"

Once they placed their order and received their food, he carried the tray to a small table that afforded him the ability to keep an eye on the front door.

Before he could open his sandwich, Melissa closed her eyes and bowed her head. "Dear Lord, we thank You for keeping us safe today, for guiding us on Your path and for this food we're about to eat. Amen."

"Amen," he and Hailey said at the same time, causing Hailey to giggle.

"How long until we get to the hunting cabin?" Melissa asked as she nibbled a french fry.

He grimaced, realizing he hadn't asked his dad for the address. He called again, but this time his father didn't pick up, no doubt because he was driving.

"It should be no more than fifteen to twenty minutes, providing I can avoid getting lost," he admitted. "I haven't been there in two years."

To his surprise, Melissa didn't seem too upset. "I'm sure you'll find it," she assured him. "You always had an excellent sense of direction, at least compared with me."

He was reminded of the time they'd taken a drive down to the beach on the shores of Lake Michigan. It wasn't difficult to find the lake as long as you headed east, but she'd kept insisting that they were headed the wrong way.

"Just because I could find my way around here doesn't mean I'll find Amelia's brother's cabin," he said drily. "Everyone else could find the lakefront, too."

"I don't know how I managed to get so turned around," she murmured. "We were late to the senior skip beach party, all because of me."

"We had a lot of fun back then," he said, momentarily lost in high school memories.

Melissa's expression softened and she glanced over as if to be sure that Hailey wasn't listening to their conversation. Fortunately she was busy coloring a picture. "We did. But we also didn't have any responsibilities."

She was right. They were both different people now than they were twelve years ago. "True. But I still missed you after you left."

Melissa's gaze darkened, and she set her chicken sandwich down as if she'd lost her appetite. "Leaving you, my home, everything I knew, was the hardest thing for me to do, Nate. You have no idea what it's like to start over in a new city without knowing anyone."

"I wish you had trusted in the system. In me," he added, knowing that was the part bothering him the most.

She shook her head. "I was young. I truly thought no one would believe me. Not even you. Not when your uncle was there that night."

Maybe she was right. It was easy to say now that he would have believed her, but would he have gone against his uncle back when he was barely eighteen? His mother had been gone for eight years by then, and he'd grown closer to his mother's brother after she'd left him and his dad.

"Mommy, can I go play?" Hailey asked, gesturing to the play set just a few yards away.

"For a few minutes, until Mr. Nate and I are finished eating."

"Goody," Hailey shouted, jumping down from the table and running over to where a couple of other kids were already playing. Nate was impressed that Hailey wasn't overly shy about joining the others.

"I hope you don't mind giving her some time to run around," Melissa said softly. "Hailey sometimes gets lonely, being an only child. Besides, we've done nothing but drive for what seems like days."

"Of course not," Nate said. He took another bite of his sandwich. "In fact, I can bring the computer in here and use the free Wi-Fi for an hour or so if you think that would help."

"Really? That would be great." Melissa's eyes brightened at his suggestion. "I want to give Hailey at least some semblance of normalcy after everything that's happened. When I think about how close that bullet came to hitting you…" Her voice trailed off.

"Hey, try not to worry about that," he urged her, reaching over to cover her hand with his. "We're going to get through this, Melissa. I'll do everything in my power to keep you and Hailey out of harm's way."

Her smile was tremulous. "I know. I have faith in you, Nate. And I have faith in God's plan. I hate feeling so helpless, though, not knowing how we're going to find the actual murderer."

"I know." He gave her fingers a gentle squeeze before releasing her. He didn't understand why he was so drawn to this more mature version of Melissa, the conscientious mother and the believer in faith and God.

She was the exact opposite from the type of woman he generally dated.

From the type of woman she'd been when they'd dated so many years ago.

Was it possible he'd been subconsciously searching for a replacement for the young, carefree girl she'd once been? Instead of moving on with his life?

It occurred to him that it might be better to stop living in the past. Watching the mother-and-daughter duo, he realized that he was tired of his usual dating scene.

Ironically he wanted something more. A home, a family.

Not with Melissa, since she'd be leaving as soon as they'd figured out who was trying to kill her and why.

But maybe with a different type of woman than he normally went out with.

Surely the right person was out there, somewhere.

Melissa's hand continued to tingle with awareness even after Nate let her go. "That was good," she said, balling up her empty wrapper and tossing it on the tray.

"Agreed. I'll be right back with the computer," Nate said, avoiding her gaze as he piled the garbage on the plastic tray.

"Sounds good." She watched as he took care of their trash on his way outside to the car. She couldn't seem to tear her gaze away. Although she normally stayed far away from cops, there was something about a guy in uniform that oozed strength, confidence and protectiveness.

All traits Nate possessed in full force.

She forced herself to look away. Turning in her seat, she swept her gaze over the area, searching for Hailey. When Melissa spotted her daughter, the little girl looked as if she was having a great time.

Suddenly she noticed something else. A dark van pulling into the parking lot.

She froze, her heart pounding with fear. Had the gunmen found them?

No, this car was blue, not green, and there was a young couple sitting in the front seat, not two menacing men. She let out a heavy sigh of relief.

When Nate returned with the computer, she shook off the feeling of doom.

She wanted to help him research the murder she'd witnessed. The sooner they discovered the identity of the man who'd been stabbed to death, the better.

Nate sat down, opened the computer and booted up the hard drive.

She scooted closer so she could see the screen. "Where on earth are you going to start looking for the victim of a twelve-year-old murder?" she asked in a whisper.

"It won't be easy, although we can start with the police database," Nate admitted. "I'm hoping that they didn't take time to bury the body and that it was found not far after the incident." He opened a document and then glanced at her questioningly. "You're sure the victim is male, correct?"

"Absolutely," she said with conviction.

"Do you remember what he looked like?"

Melissa braced her head in her hands and closed her eyes, putting herself back in the restaurant as she'd served their table. She'd waited on them often enough that the image was fairly clear. "He was roughly six feet tall with blond hair that was long, almost to his shoulders, giving him a bit of a surfer look."

Nate took notes. "Do you have an approximate age? And what he was wearing?"

She shrugged helplessly. "Age is going to be difficult. You know everyone looked old to us back then. But in comparison with your uncle Tom? I'd say roughly the same age, maybe a little younger."

Nate pursed his lips. "My uncle is the same age as my dad, fifty-five, and my mom was two years younger. So twelve years ago, Tom would have been forty-three."

"That sounds about right," Melissa agreed. "The man who died was dressed more casually than the others, as if he didn't quite belong."

"What do you mean, casually?" Nate asked.

"He wore dress slacks and polo shirts, compared with your uncle, who always wore very expensive suits and shirts with his initials embroidered on the cuffs."

"I'd almost forgotten that detail," Nate murmured with a frown. "Okay, anything else stand out in your memory?"

Melissa had relived the night of the stabbing about a hundred times in her mind. "I remember that the blond surfer guy wasn't always included in the conversations. Sometimes he just sat there, listening."

"What kind of conversations?"

"Politics, mostly. To be honest, I never paid that much attention to what they discussed, since that topic didn't interest me. Although they did talk about money a lot, too."

Nate lifted a brow. "Money? Anything more specific?"

"Campaign contributions," she said slowly. Bits and pieces of the conversations were coming back to her. "Something about how to protect the income from campaign contributions."

"That seems strange, if the only elected official there was my uncle Tom," he said thoughtfully.

"Not just your uncle. I seem to remember that the blond surfer guy also talked about his campaign contributions on occasion."

"Bingo," Nate muttered under his breath as he opened a search engine. "Knowing the dead guy was an elected official should help narrow our search."

Melissa knew how to use graphics to create designs, but watching Nate's fingers fly over the keyboard made her realize he was no slouch when it came to computers, either.

A high-pitched cry made her leap to her feet. "Hailey?" she called, rushing over to the play center.

"I bumped my head," her daughter whimpered, rubbing a spot on the side of her temple.

"Let me see," she said, gently probing the area. There was a slight bump, but the skin wasn't broken. "Come sit at the table. I'll get you some ice."

"I'll grab some ice for you," one of the other mothers offered helpfully.

"Thanks." She carried Hailey back to the table where Nate was waiting, a concerned expression in his brown eyes.

"Is she okay?"

Melissa nodded. "Just a bump on her head. Nothing serious." She took the ice from the mother of the little girl Hailey had been playing with. "Thanks."

She pressed the cold napkin against Hailey's temple for a few minutes, which was as long as her daughter would sit still.

"It's too cold, Mommy," Hailey said, pushing her hand away.

"But the ice will make it feel better," she pointed out. "Just a little while longer, okay?"

Hailey tolerated the ice for another three minutes before wiggling off her lap. "Can I play some more?"

Melissa hesitated, glancing over at Nate. "How much longer do you need?"

"Thirty minutes would be great, but if you want to leave now, that's okay, too."

"Thirty more minutes, please?" Hailey asked, the bump on her head clearly forgotten.

"All right, but be careful, okay?" Melissa watched with exasperation as her daughter ran back to the play set, knowing that it was better for Hailey to burn off a little more energy before they had to get back in the car again.

She wasn't sure what to expect at the cabin. Did it even have electricity and running water? She sincerely hoped so. Not that she could afford to be picky.

"Melissa, come here and take a look at these photographs," Nate said, drawing her attention back to the issue at hand. "Tell me if you recognize any of these men."

She went over to sit beside him so she could see the computer screen. "That's your uncle Tom," she said, pointing to the man standing in the center of the group.

"Yeah, I know. What about the others?"

She stared at the screen for a long moment. "I'm sorry, but none of the others look familiar."

Nate grimaced. "I was wondering if this blond guy here might be the same one you saw that night. He has short hair in this picture, but it was taken a year before we graduated from high school."

She leaned closer, trying to imagine the guy with longer hair. "I'm sorry, but I just can't say for sure."

"Okay, I'll keep looking."

Melissa caught a glimpse of the titles listed in the

caption beneath the picture. "Wait a minute. These are all city aldermen?"

"Yes, why?"

The memory clicked into place. "I remember your uncle referring to the blond guy as an alderman. Oh, if only I could remember his last name."

"If he's an alderman, I can narrow the search even further," Nate said with satisfaction.

She waited patiently as he typed commands into the search engine and watched as Hailey and the other girl took turns going down the slide.

"Here we go," Nate muttered. He turned the computer so that she could see the screen without any glare from the sunlight. "Scroll through these. See if anyone looks familiar."

She did as he asked, taking her time with each photograph. Three pages down, she gasped at the familiar face on the screen.

"That's him," she whispered. "That's the man who was stabbed that night."

"Alderman Kevin Turner," Nate said in a low voice. "He was the alderman of our district, the one where I grew up. In fact, my dad still lives in the area, although he moved into a smaller house once I moved away. Back when I was younger, Kevin Turner lived directly across the street from us."

Melissa shivered, thinking about the irony of the situation. The interpersonal relationships back then were too close for comfort. "I guess now that we have a name, we can verify when and how he died."

"Absolutely. Just give me another couple of minutes here." Nate turned the computer back toward himself and went to work. For several long moments, there was nothing but the tapping of his fingers to break the silence.

"Here it is," Nate said. "Alderman Kevin Turner, died on June 16 from a stab wound in a brutal mugging in Milwaukee."

"Milwaukee?" Melissa scowled. "That's not true. He died in Brookmont."

"Unfortunately, it won't be very easy to prove otherwise," Nate murmured.

She read the article twice, the old, familiar sense of dread seeping into her stomach.

These men had covered their tracks exceedingly well. Finding the victim hadn't helped reveal the truth about what happened that night and why.

In fact, she was beginning to believe that the men involved had the money and power to do whatever they wanted.

Including the ability to get away with murder.

# EIGHT

Nate battled a wave of helplessness. In his heart he knew that Kevin Turner was the victim Melissa had watched die twelve years ago, but proving that fact was something else entirely.

Yeah, sure, they had Melissa as an eyewitness, but they needed forensic evidence to support their theory. Something more than the word of a girl who'd had drugs found in her room and who'd disappeared, then faked her death.

The biggest issue was motive. Why on earth had Kevin Turner been murdered?

"This doesn't help us one bit, does it?" Melissa said in a dull, flat tone.

The listlessness in her voice bothered him, spurring a sense of determination. "It's the first step in uncovering the truth," he said firmly. "We know that money was involved, be it campaign funds or otherwise. We'll just need to find out more about this Kevin Turner. And to understand why he was murdered that night. From what you described, it doesn't seem as if he was killed in a fit of anger."

"I'm really not sure," Melissa said with sigh. "It looked

like they were just talking when suddenly the guy next to your uncle pulled out a knife and stabbed him."

"So it could have been a crime of opportunity," Nate mused half to himself.

"Maybe we're kidding ourselves, Nate. We could dig into this for days and still not know exactly what happened."

"Hey, you're not giving up on me, are you?" he asked gently. He hated seeing the dull, resigned expression in her hazel eyes. "Aren't you the one who told me to have faith?"

"Yes," she acknowledged with a self-deprecating smile. "You're right. Sometimes I still struggle with it. Especially now. I feel like every time we try to take a step forward, we're given a massive shove backward."

"But we're still on our feet," Nate said encouragingly. "And that means we're still fighting."

Her smile widened. "Okay, yes, we're still fighting. And since someone is trying to silence us once and for all, there just might be something they're afraid we'll find out. Something that will lead us to the truth."

"That's my girl," he said, enjoying the way she blushed. "I hate to leave, but we should probably get back on the road. I'd prefer to reach the cabin before it gets too dark."

"Sounds good," Melissa agreed. "I'll get Hailey."

Nate nodded as he quickly shut down the computer and glanced at his watch. From what he remembered, Amelia's brother's cabin had the basics—water, nonperishable food and electricity—but he couldn't be sure there was any computer access.

Too late to consider stopping at a store to purchase a satellite modem, even if he was willing to use up a good chunk of his cash, which wouldn't be smart. No, he'd have to make do with going to public places that offered free services as needed.

"Goodbye, Sally," Hailey said, waving to her new-found friend.

"'Bye, Hailey."

"That was so fun," the little girl declared as they walked outside to the car. "Can I see Sally again, Mommy?"

Melissa's smile was strained. "We'll see."

"'We'll see' means no," Hailey muttered, obviously disappointed.

Nate felt bad for her. It couldn't be easy to be so far away from her friends, especially less than a week before Christmas. Obviously keeping her safe was more important, but that didn't make him feel any better.

If things were normal, he could take Melissa and Hailey to visit his teammate Caleb, his wife, Noelle, and their daughter, Kaitlin. He was sure the girls would get along great.

Caleb and Noelle had recently been blessed with a son they'd christened Anthony. Seeing the expression on Caleb's face when he stared down at his son had filled Nate with an odd sense of longing.

Having a family seemed a distant dream. Especially considering his own upbringing. His mother had left when he was ten years old, never once talking to him or even sending a letter. She certainly hadn't missed him.

He remembered overhearing his parents arguing but had never thought too much about it. All parents fought sometimes, didn't they?

But one day he came home from school to find there was no one home. He'd called his dad in a panic, and for a short time, they'd feared his mother had been taken against her will.

Until they realized all her clothes were gone.

For months after, he'd wondered if his parents had been fighting over him. If he'd done something that had caused his mother to leave.

"Nate? Are you okay?"

He realized he'd been sitting and staring blankly through the windshield, lost in the memories. "Uh, yeah, I'm fine," he said gruffly. "I'm just trying to remember the route to the cabin."

That much was partially true. Nate drove out of the parking lot and headed north. "Are there any landmarks that I can help look for?" Melissa asked.

"First we have to find Highway 44," he said. "The town the cabin is located in is called New Haven, and it's not far off the highway. Unfortunately, I can't think of the street name."

"I'm sure you'll recognize it when you see it," she said.

He sure hoped so.

Neither of them said much for the next few miles. He was thinking about turning around when Melissa leaned forward excitedly. "Hey, there's a highway sign up ahead."

"Junction 44," Nate read out loud, relieved he'd been on the right track. He slowed down and then turned left so they were headed west.

"I'll read the street names out loud," Melissa offered.

He listened as they passed one intersection and then another. So far, neither street sounded familiar. Nate grew tense as he concentrated on navigating in the deepening dusk. And found himself silently praying for God's help in remembering the way. How did Melissa phrase it?

*Dear Lord, please guide me on Your path. Amen.*

Instantly he felt more calm and relaxed. Maybe it was

all in his head, but since he'd met her, he'd begun to realize that leaning on the power of prayer could help a person get through difficult times.

"Turkey Hollow," Melissa said, breaking into his thoughts.

"That's it!" Nate exclaimed. "That's the road that will take us to Lake Point Drive."

"That means we're almost there, right Mommy?" Hailey asked from the backseat.

"That's right." Melissa reached over to touch his hand, and he glanced at her questioningly. "What sort of cabin is this?" she asked in a low tone. "I'd like to prepare Hailey if we're going to be camping out."

He grinned and shook his head. "No need to worry. The cabin has running water and electricity. I just can't remember if there was computer access or not. The last time I was here, I spent most of the time fishing on the lake with my dad."

"You and your father were always very close," Melissa murmured. "Just like me and my dad were."

"Yeah, we were. After my mother left, we learned to lean on each other a lot. I was angry with him at first, but then one night I found him crying, and that really shook me. I'd always thought of my dad as a tough firefighter, and I'd never, ever seen him cry."

"Oh, Nate, that must have been so hard."

He shifted in his seat, uncomfortable with her sympathy. "That's all in the past now. It's no big deal. My dad and I have only got closer over the years. He finally remarried after I graduated from college, to a very nice lady who makes him happy."

"And you've never heard from your mother since the day she left?" Melissa asked.

"No." He didn't want to talk about that now. He gestured toward the windshield. "Help me look for Lake Point Drive. I'm pretty sure that will take us to the cabin."

"All right," she agreed.

Nate was glad she'd dropped the subject of his mother. Why was he wasting his time now thinking about the woman who'd left him? There was no point. He needed to stay focused on investigating a twelve-year-old murder.

And if watching Melissa interact with her daughter reminded him of the mother he'd missed, that was nobody's problem but his own.

Melissa sensed she'd struck a nerve asking about Nate's mother. Even back when they were dating their senior year of high school, he'd refused to talk about her.

She hadn't appreciated what Nate had really gone through until she'd given birth to Hailey. How any mother could willingly give up her child was beyond her realm of comprehension.

"There's Lake Point Drive," she said in case Nate hadn't noticed. "Right or left?"

"We'll head left, although I think the road completely encircles the lake," he said. "So we should be able to find the cabin."

"Is it right off this road?" Melissa frowned when they passed a cross street. "There seem to be a couple of cul-de-sacs along the way."

"No, it's not on a cul-de-sac," he said. "I remember it seemed to be surrounded completely by trees, giving it a sense of isolation, with a nice view of the lake. So it has to be off to the right side of the road."

Melissa nodded and stayed alert for possibilities. She

estimated they'd gone halfway around the lake before Nate slowed down.

"Found it," he said as he turned onto a snow-covered driveway. Thankfully the snow wasn't too deep, so the car was able to make it all the way up to the structure.

Although it looked more like a cottage than a cabin. The wood siding was gold in color, blending nicely with the trees, with green trim and green shutters. There was no garage, and she could see a glimpse of the lake, which appeared to be frozen solid.

"Why don't you wait here for a minute?" Nate suggested. "I'll get the door open and turn on the lights so you can see."

"All right." She waited patiently with Hailey as he dug around for the key and let himself inside. Less than ten minutes later, there was a welcoming glow illuminating from the windows, and Nate returned to the car.

He grabbed the computer case, his duffel and her suitcase, leaving her to walk with Hailey.

"Look, Mommy, lots and lots of pretty white snow!" There was a good two feet here, double what had been on the ground in Milwaukee. Her daughter ran over to scoop up a handful and tossed it in the air. "Can we build a snowman? Can we?"

"Yes, but not now. It's too dark. We'll make one in the morning, okay?"

For a moment Hailey wavered, as if she wanted to press the issue, but then she nodded and joined Melissa at the door.

"Wow, this is nice," she said as she stepped inside. The interior was warm and cozy, nothing at all like she'd expected. A comfortable leather sofa and love seat were set up in front of a fireplace, and the kitchen had several decent amenities, including a stove, refrigerator and microwave. "Not as rustic as I imagined."

"Best of all, I see there's wireless internet access," Nate said as he set the computer case on the oak kitchen table. "Unfortunately, there's not much food, but if you give me a list of things you'd like, I'll run to the general store."

"Okay," Melissa agreed. She wrote down some basic food items that Hailey preferred and handed it to Nate.

"Make yourself at home," Nate said as he headed toward the door. "You and Hailey will want to share the master bedroom. I'll use the guest room."

She nodded and busied herself with unpacking their small suitcase. The so-called cabin was larger than her two-bedroom apartment, yet cozy at the same time.

Nate returned twenty minutes later and they worked at throwing together a quick beef stew for dinner.

Melissa felt a little off balance with Nate so close, but she needn't have worried. As soon as they'd finished their meal and cleaned up the dirty dishes, he sat down and retreated behind his computer.

She searched around for something for Hailey to do, and when she found an old game of Chutes and Ladders, her daughter was delighted to take her on.

They played until Hailey's eyelids began to droop. "Come on. Time to brush your teeth and get into bed."

She didn't argue the way she normally did, and Melissa was even more surprised when she didn't have to remind her daughter to say her prayers.

"God bless Daddy, Mommy, my new friend Sally and Mr. Nate. Amen."

"Amen," Melissa murmured.

"Amen," Nate said from the doorway behind her, making her jump.

She glanced around in surprise, but then leaned down to give Hailey a hug and a kiss. "Good night, sweetie."

"Good night, Mommy. Good night, Mr. Nate."

Melissa walked toward Nate, trying not to be annoyed that her daughter kept including him in her prayers. It wasn't as if Nate could ever replace Hailey's real father.

She gave herself a mental shake. What was wrong with her? She should be glad that Hailey had someone like Nate to protect her.

"Find anything more about Kevin Turner?" she asked, anxious to veer her thoughts elsewhere.

"No, but I was wondering if you could take a few minutes to look at more photos, see if you can identify any of the other men who were at the scene of the crime that night."

"Sure." She brushed past Nate to return to the kitchen, the woodsy scent of his aftershave filling her head.

It took several minutes for her to scroll through the images. When she got to a group shot, she increased the size of the picture so she could study their faces.

"This guy here," she said, tapping her finger on the screen. "He's the cop who was there that night."

"Randall Joseph?" Nate asked in a shocked tone. "Are you absolutely sure?"

She looked again and nodded. "I'm sure. That's him. Why are you so surprised? Because he's still a cop?"

"Not just that," Nate said slowly, a grim expression in his eyes. "Randall Joseph is the Brookmont chief of police."

"The chief of police? Are you serious?" She stared at Nate in horror and then abruptly jumped up from the chair, knocking it over in her haste to get away. "That's just perfect. He's in charge of all the police officers.

There's no way in the world anyone will believe my story now."

Nate righted the chair, eyeing her warily. "Calm down, Melissa."

"Calm down?" Frustration welled in her chest to the point that she felt as if she might explode. "How can I calm down? As if having the mayor involved wasn't bad enough, now we have the chief of police, too? What's next? A judge? The state governor?"

She knew her voice was rising and she was losing control, but she couldn't seem to get a grip. The odds were overwhelmingly stacked against them. She and Hailey might never be safe.

Ever!

"Shh, it's okay." Nate was there, gathering her into his arms and pulling her tightly against him. For a moment she wanted to pummel him with her fists, but then she buried her face in his shoulder, breathing in his familiar scent. She squeezed her eyes shut, trying to keep the tears that threatened at bay.

"Oh, Nate, what are we going to do?" she whispered, her voice muffled against his shirt.

"We're going to get to get to the bottom of this crime," Nate said grimly. "No one is infallible. And you said it earlier. They're coming after us because they're afraid we'll succeed in uncovering their dirty little secrets."

She desperately wanted to believe that. It wasn't like her to lose faith like this. But losing her father and being in danger were wearing her down. She relaxed against Nate, soaking up some of his strength. It felt good to be in his arms.

Too good.

Reluctantly, she pulled herself together and eased

away from him, swiping at her damp eyes. "Sorry about that," she said. "I'm okay now."

"You don't have to apologize to me," he said, lifting a hand to brush a strand of her hair off her cheek. His touch was feather-light, yet she felt the ripples down to the soles of her feet. "I believe the truth will prevail. These guys are probably right now trying to find a way to find us, determined to keep their crime hidden in the past."

Melissa nodded, imagining these men sitting at the restaurant the way they used to, talking in low tones among themselves. "Wait a minute. That's it!"

"What?" Nate asked, clearly confused.

"The restaurant, El Matador. You said it's still there, right?" When Nate nodded, she rushed on. "What are the chances that these guys still eat dinner there?"

Realization dawned in Nate's eyes. "I'd say pretty good."

"Exactly." Melissa couldn't believe she hadn't thought of this before. "Why couldn't we go there and see if we can overhear what they're saying? I could disguise myself, dye my hair red or wear a pair of thick-framed glasses. I could even dress up like a server, although I'm sure their uniforms have changed."

"Not an option," Nate said in a flat tone. "They'll probably still recognize you. But you might be onto something. We could use cameras and hidden microphones to find out what they're talking about."

"Really? You can do that?" she asked in amazement.

"Yeah, although we'll need some help getting the equipment," Nate said thoughtfully. "I'll give Jenna a call tomorrow, see what we can come up with."

"Good." Melissa longed to move back into Nate's

arms, so she forced herself to take a step away from the temptation and to focus on their next steps.

Maybe the task of bringing down a chief of police and the Brookmont mayor wasn't as ridiculous as it sounded.

She was beginning to believe that with Nate at her side, anything was possible.

# NINE

Sleep eluded him, causing Nate to toss and turn, his thoughts spinning in circles as he ruminated over the mystery of Alderman Turner's murder. Eventually he gave up, dragging himself out of bed early in the morning. The cabin was quiet, and he found himself glad that Melissa and Hailey were still asleep.

He needed some quiet time to come to grips with the fact that his uncle Tom was involved in something criminal. More than just covering up a murder, as if that wasn't bad enough. The motive for killing Turner had to have been big enough to take the risk of getting caught. And for all he knew, his uncle was still involved in whatever illegal activities had led to the murder in the first place.

After getting dressed in the comfortable jeans and sweatshirt that he'd found packed in his duffel and securing his weapon in deference to Hailey, he padded into the kitchen to make some coffee. Waiting for the pot to brew, he stared out the window, squinting at how the sun reflected blindingly off the snow.

Another beautiful day out, but all he could think of was that this was just another day closer to Christmas. It didn't seem fair that Hailey should have to be here, hiding in a remote lakeside cabin over the holiday. He needed to step up the investigation, to get the proof he needed to convince Griff to take a chance on continuing the case as soon as possible.

Nate filled up a large mug with steaming black coffee and headed over to the table where he'd left his computer. He created a new email address and then wrote a note to Jenna, asking her to bring him the electronic supplies he needed from his house.

Too bad he hadn't thought about this before now. He hated the idea of Jenna having to sneak past whoever was staked outside his place once again. And unfortunately his gadgets were stored all over the living space, so she'd have to search around to find everything he needed.

If he didn't hear from her in a couple of hours, he could finally charge up one of the new disposable cell phones and call her.

Sipping his coffee, he began to search further back in time in order to figure out what Alderman Turner might have been involved in. Not an easy task, but Nate knew how to make the most of the technology he had at his fingertips.

"Good morning." Melissa's soft, husky voice startled him so badly he spilled coffee on his jeans.

"Uh, hi," he said awkwardly, turning in his seat to face her. How was it possible that she looked so beautiful first thing in the morning, even with sleep-tousled hair and no makeup?

"Thanks for making coffee," she murmured, heading straight over to the pot. "I'll get breakfast started. Anything you're craving in particular?"

He didn't want her to feel as if she needed to cook for him, and he was about to offer to do it himself when Hailey bounded into the room.

"Can we build a snowman, Mommy? Can we?"

"After breakfast," Melissa said with an indulgent smile. "What would you like? Oatmeal or eggs?"

"Oatmeal," Hailey said, jumping up and down with excitement. "I want oatmeal."

"Works for me," Nate said, pushing the computer off to the side and then rising to his feet. "I'll make it."

"No, no, I'll do it," Melissa said hastily. "Just sit down. You're working, and I don't know how to search the internet the way you do."

He sank back down, making a mental note to do the dishes afterward. Even as he continued to search, he was distracted by Hailey's chatter.

Melissa was patient and kind, allowing Hailey to stand on a chair to help stir the oatmeal. He couldn't help comparing her to his own absent mother.

Nate vaguely remembered making Christmas cookies with his mom one time. In fact, she'd scolded him for eating too many and making himself sick. He couldn't recall what she'd looked like that day, but surely there must have been other tender moments they'd shared.

Too bad he couldn't think of anything specific.

No sense in dwelling on that now. He went back to the case at hand, but so far he hadn't found out much about Kevin Turner. He was tempted to ask his dad what he remembered since they'd lived just across the street, but he doubted that old neighborhood memories would be much help.

"Thanks," he said when Melissa set a steaming bowl of oatmeal down on the table. She and Hailey sat and then bowed their heads to pray.

"Dear Lord," Melissa said, "we thank You for this food and shelter. We also ask for Your continued protection and guidance as we continue to seek the truth. Amen."

"Amen," he said, appreciating the content of her prayer.

"Dig in," Hailey said with enthusiasm as she added brown sugar and raisins to her bowl. It was weird being together like this, as if they were a family.

But they weren't. A fact he needed to remember.

"Have you thought about our plan to go back to the restaurant?" Melissa asked.

"Yeah, I sent Jenna an email with a list of supplies that we'll need. I don't like making her go back to my place again, but it's better than trying to buy everything new. I haven't heard from her yet, though."

"You have cameras and listening devices at your house?" she asked in surprise.

He could feel the tips of his ears burning with embarrassment. Could he sound like a bigger nerd? Probably not. "I happen to like electronics," he mumbled. "Mmm, this oatmeal is really good."

She didn't ask anything more, and as soon as they were finished eating, he jumped up to do the dishes. "You cooked. My turn to clean up," he insisted.

"Let's go outside, Mommy!" Hailey pleaded with wide hazel eyes. "Please?"

"Take her outside. I'll wash the dishes and continue working," Nate said firmly.

Melissa hesitated, and when her gaze met his, he was struck by the fact that she'd expected him to come outside with them. And while the thought was tempting, he had work to do.

At least, that's what he told himself. But as he finished drying the plates, watching as Hailey and Melissa laughed and played, building a snowman in the front yard, Nate knew that he'd insisted on staying inside to prevent himself from getting too close.

He settled down behind the computer, determined to find something that would help. After some more digging he discovered that both Kevin Turner and his uncle, Tom McAllister, ran for office at the same time, roughly six years before the murder. Then they were also re-elected four years later.

Had they made some sort of pact back then? Obviously they'd both received campaign contributions, but were some of them illegal? Or worse, did they use the campaign funds as a way to hide dirty money? Like from drugs?

The idea of his uncle Tom being involved in something illegal was deeply disturbing, but he also couldn't deny the fact there were drugs planted in Melissa's room to discredit her story. Were those narcotics part of their scheme? Unfortunately, the connection seemed to make sense.

Nate had no idea how much time had passed, but just as Melissa and Hailey came back in, he found a bunch of campaign celebration photographs from the second election.

He scrolled through the pictures and then stopped abruptly as a large group photo bloomed on the screen. He stared at it in shock.

"Nate?" Melissa's voice was faint, as if she were speaking through a thick blanket. "Nate! Are you all right?"

No, he wasn't all right. His chest hurt as he struggled to breathe.

"What did you find?" Melissa crossed over and leaned against his shoulder. "That's Alderman Kevin

Turner," she said, pointing at the man standing off to the side. "Who's the woman he's talking to?"

The band around his chest finally loosened enough for Nate to respond. "That's my mother, Rosalie Freemont."

Melissa caught her breath at Nate's terse admission. His mother? The woman who'd abandoned him and his father? She found herself leaning closer, trying to get a good look at her.

Rosalie was stunningly beautiful. Her hair was darker than Nate's sandy color, but they shared many of the same facial features, and it was easy to see where Nate had inherited his good looks. But she couldn't help thinking that the closeness between Nate's mother and Alderman Turner was far too cozy for comfort, especially since there was no mention of Nate's father.

"I wonder if she knew that this picture was taken," Nate said in a low tone.

"I'm sorry," she said, putting a soothing arm around his shoulders. It couldn't be easy to come face-to-face with a painful part of his past.

"No need to apologize," he said gruffly, pushing away from the computer and breaking away from her embrace. He stood and began to pace. "Fact is, I barely even remembered what she looked like until I saw the photograph."

"I lost my mother to a brain aneurysm," Melissa said. "It was a total shock. One minute she's alive and talking. The next she was gone. Not like my father, who knew he had cancer and that he only had a few months to live."

"I'm sure that was terrible for you, but at least your mother didn't leave voluntarily," Nate said.

"Do you know that for sure?" she pressed. "Isn't it possible something awful happened to her?"

"No. In fact, my uncle Tom told me and my dad that she was living out in Arizona. Even with that news, my dad didn't initiate divorce proceedings until I was in college. He asked Tom to get them to my mother, and they were returned with her signature on them."

"That's awful, Nate," Melissa said, her heart breaking for him. No little boy should have to go through something like that. Why couldn't his mother have tried to stay in touch?

"Never mind that now," Nate said with an impatient wave of his hand. "I still haven't heard from Jenna about getting the technology we need to bug the restaurant. I'll try calling her with one of the disposable phones."

"I just looked at mine, and there's only one bar, so I'm not sure we'll get service up here," Melissa said with a sigh.

Nate looked at his phone and scowled. She watched as he tried to call Jenna, only to receive an error message. Tossing his device aside, he crossed back over to the computer. "I'll try one more email, but if that doesn't work, my regular cell gets better service so I'll have no choice but to use it."

She followed him and was relieved to see that Jenna had responded. "What did she say?"

Nate read Jenna's message out loud. "'Happy to help, but have no clue what any of this stuff looks like. I'll distract the guys watching the place so you can go in and get what you need.'"

Melissa straightened and glanced at him. "Are you sure that's a good idea?" She hated the thought of Nate putting himself in danger.

She read over his shoulder as he typed a response.

Sounds like a plan. What time can we meet?

Jenna quickly replied back.

I swapped for a day shift today, so how about when I'm off work, maybe around 4:30? I'll meet you at my place.

Sounds good. See you then.

Nate sent off his reply, and once again, Melissa squashed a flash of jealousy. He'd made a point of explaining that he and Jenna were friends and colleagues, nothing more. So why did the familiarity between them bother her?

Quite honestly, it shouldn't.

"So, what should we do in the meantime?" Melissa asked.

Nate glanced at his watch. "I'm sure Hailey needs to eat lunch soon, right?" When she nodded in agreement, he continued, "We're almost two hours from Brookmont, so we'll head in as soon as we finish eating."

"All right," she agreed. "It wouldn't hurt to drive past the restaurant to see if anyone is there who we recognize."

"I think that's a good idea. I really don't like dragging you and Hailey with me, but I'm not sure that leaving you here alone is a good option."

"I'd rather go with you," she said hastily. "Between the two of us, I'm sure we can protect Hailey."

Nate nodded, but there was a troubled expression in his eyes as if he had doubts about the plan.

Too bad. No way was she letting him go off on his own, leaving her and Hailey here to wonder what was going on.

Melissa draped Hailey's hat, scarf and mittens around the heat vent near the floor so they would be dry by

**W**e'd like to send you two free books from the series you are enjoying now. Your two books have a combined cover price of over $10, but are yours to keep absolutely FREE! We'll even send you two wonderful surprise gifts. You can't lose!

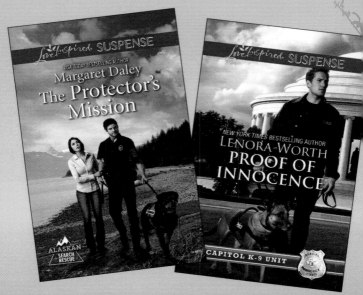

Each of your FREE books is filled with joy, faith and traditional values and women open their hearts to each other and join together on a spir journey.

Visit us at
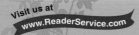
www.ReaderService.com

# GET 2 FREE BOOKS!

## HURRY!
**Return this card today to get 2 FREE Books and 2 FREE Bonus Gifts!**

**YES!** Please send me the **2 FREE books** and **2 FREE gifts** for which I qualify. I understand that I am under no obligation to purchase anything further, as explained on the back of this card.

**PLACE FREE GIFTS SEAL HERE**

❏ I prefer the regular-print edition
153/353 IDL GHP6

❏ I prefer the larger-print edition
107/307 IDL GHUJ

FIRST NAME

LAST NAME

ADDRESS

APT.#

CITY

STATE/PROV.

ZIP/POSTAL CODE

SLI-N15-IV15

## READER SERVICE—**Here's how it works:**

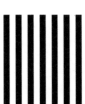

the time they needed to leave. Then they played another game of Chutes and Ladders before heading back into the kitchen to make soup and sandwiches for lunch. She'd been touched by the fact that Nate had insisted on cleaning up the breakfast dishes. She hadn't had anyone helping her with the chores since Jeremy died.

Although if she were honest, Jeremy hadn't really helped out in the kitchen much. He was a good man, and she believed he'd have been a great father, even though he hadn't been given that chance.

She remembered praying in church those first few months after his death as she'd grown large with his child, trying to make sense of God's plan. Her pastor had helped a lot, but it wasn't until now that she realized maybe this was all happening just the way God intended.

Had He brought her and Nate together for a reason? Something other than finding out about the murder she'd witnessed?

She'd been disappointed that Nate hadn't joined them outside, assuming that it was more than just working on the investigation that had kept him away.

Despite how great he was with Hailey, she didn't get the sense that he relished the idea of being a role model for her daughter. Which was a little odd, considering that he had a great relationship with his dad.

"I'll clean up," Nate said when they'd finished their meal.

"We'll finish faster if we do it together," she pointed out. "Hailey, why don't you get your handheld computer game for the car ride?"

"Okay," Hailey agreed. The little girl disappeared into the bedroom to fetch what she needed.

Nate didn't say much as he washed the dishes. She

placed the leftover soup in the fridge before picking up the dish towel to begin drying.

"Do you really think using the cameras and microphones will work?" she asked in an effort to break the strained silence.

"I hope so," Nate said in a grim tone. "We need something more to go on. Finding the man who'd been murdered didn't help as much as I'd hoped."

"I know," she agreed with a sigh. "I wonder if the interior of the restaurant has changed over time."

Nate shrugged. "They renovated the kitchen a few years back, but I think the layout of the dining room is basically the same."

"That will help," she murmured. She could already envision the best places to plant the cameras and listening devices.

But first they needed to get the equipment out of Nate's house.

The time was close to one thirty before they were on the road, heading back toward civilization. The two-hour drive seemed to fly by as their car ate up the miles. Nate exited the interstate and took side streets until they reached the restaurant.

Melissa twisted her fingers together as he first drove past the restaurant and then circled around to pull into the parking lot.

He sat there for a moment, staring out through the windshield.

She put her hand on his arm. "What's wrong?"

"That's my uncle's car," Nate said, gesturing to an expensive SUV parked near the front door. "I assume some of the others are here, too. Unfortunately, I don't know what the chief of police drives these days. You were right. They must still meet here on a regular basis."

She wasn't sure what to say to make him feel better. And she thought it was creepy that these men were still holding meetings here. Did that mean whatever criminal activities they were involved in had continued over the years? The thought made her feel sick.

After several long minutes, Nate put the vehicle in Reverse and backed out of the parking lot. "Looks like we'll get there early," she said, attempting to lighten things up.

"Yeah, I know." He drove toward the meeting point, showing her his place along the way. Melissa was dismayed to realize just how close to his female coworker he lived.

Jenna joined them about twenty minutes later, earlier than they'd originally planned. Nate got out of the car and went over to talk to her, while Melissa tried to be patient.

She was glad to see that they seemed to be all business, speaking only for a few minutes before Nate came jogging back to the car.

"I need you to drive," he said, opening the passenger-side door and holding out the keys. "Jenna will give us a few minutes to get in position before confronting the vehicle that's parked a few doors down from my place."

"Okay." Melissa took the keys and slid out to go around to the driver's side. She adjusted the seat for her shorter legs and then followed Nate's directions to the street behind his place.

"I want you to drive around for about five minutes," Nate said as he slid out of the seat. "My house is right behind this white one. It won't take me long to get what I need. I'll meet you back here, okay?"

"Got it." She forced a smile, glad that thanks to the

winter solstice, darkness was already starting to fall. Within moments Nate disappeared into the shadows.

Melissa gripped the steering wheel tightly as she drove, committing the street names to memory. The five-minute drive seemed to drag on forever, but soon she pulled up to the curb where she'd dropped Nate off.

Her heart pounded with nervousness as she peered out, searching for Nate. It was probably a good thing that the windows in the white house that butted up against Nate's were dark, indicating no one was home. But where was he? Had Jenna's diversion worked? What if he'd been caught?

Melissa belatedly realized that there was no way for Nate—or Jenna, for that matter—to get in touch with her if something bad had happened. She had her disposable phone, but neither one of them had the number.

One minute ticked by and then another. Her stomach tightened with concern.

Where in the world was Nate?

# TEN

Moving quickly and silently, Nate grabbed a duffel bag and then gathered all the cameras, listening devices and receivers he needed. He didn't have his gadgets well organized, but fortunately he knew exactly where everything was located.

When he walked past the front window, he caught a glimpse of Jenna standing beside a parked car along the curb. She stood right in front of the driver's side window, effectively blocking the occupant's view of the house.

Relieved that her diversion tactic appeared to be working, he made one last sweep of the place, trying to think of what else he might need. Since he was here, he tossed more clothing in the bag, along with the spare cash he had stored in his father's watch case.

Satisfied that he wouldn't need to return anytime soon, Nate turned to leave his bedroom, the jam-packed duffel slung over his shoulder, when he heard a loud banging on the front door.

His heart jumped into his throat, and he melted back into the shadows of the bedroom, trying to understand what had happened.

"Police! Come out with your hands up!"

What? Had they seen him moving around inside?

Nate quickly considered his options. He could stay and face the police since this was, after all, his house, but he didn't trust this situation. The cops outside his door were more likely to arrest him for attempted murder for shooting those guys at the mall, or for harboring a fugitive, than to help him.

No, a better option was to make a break out the back door, but what if they'd managed to have his house surrounded?

He'd have to take his chances. While he listened to their attempts to break in his door, Nate held his weapon ready as he darted through the kitchen and opened the back door.

He barely noticed the cold air as he rushed outside into the darkness of his backyard. He'd taken only a couple of steps when the dark figure of a man emerged from the shadows to his left. "Freeze!"

His heart thudded in his chest as he imagined the weapon that was trained on him. But he refused to go down without a fight. Nate swung the duffel at the guy, hitting him square in the chest and knocking him off balance.

He managed to hang on to the bag, and then ran, darting between the trees, mentally braced for the sound of gunfire.

He covered the area between the houses in seconds, hating the fact that he was leaving footprints in the snow behind him. Just as he hit the driveway belonging to the white house, mere yards from the car where Melissa was waiting, he heard loud shouting behind him. "Back here! He's getting away!"

He yanked open the passenger door. "Go, go!"

Melissa floored the gas pedal, tires squealing as she pulled away from the curb. He managed to get the passenger door closed and fumbled with the seat belt, impressed by the way she took a quick right and then another left, zigzagging her way through the neighborhood in an effort to make sure no one was following them. Thankfully, the crazy driving didn't wake Hailey up from her deep slumber.

Several long minutes passed before he broke the silence. "Head out onto the interstate. There's plenty of traffic, so we should be able to blend in."

"Okay, but tell me what happened." Melissa's gaze was glued to the road, her fingers gripping the steering wheel tightly, making him realize that she'd been afraid on his behalf. "How did they find you?"

"I'm not sure," he said honestly. "I could see Jenna standing next to a car parked on the road, but a few minutes later there was banging on the door, and the police were demanding that I come out. One of them was waiting for me in the backyard, too."

Melissa glanced briefly at him, shock evident on her features. "They saw you inside the house?"

"Either that, or they just assumed Jenna showed up for a reason and decided to take the chance on confronting me." The more he thought about it, the more likely that scenario seemed. They must have considered Jenna's confrontation suspicious.

"How did you get away?"

He glanced down at his duffel bag with a grimace. "I hit the guy with my bag. Hope I didn't break anything."

"That was too close," Melissa muttered.

Nate couldn't help but agree. "I guess this means we're both officially fugitives from the law," he said, trying to lighten the somber mood.

"That's not funny," she said in a low voice. "Maybe we should change our names and disappear, never to be heard from again. I hate knowing I dragged you into this."

He shook his head and reached over to take her hand. "Melissa, I was the one who followed you through the mall, remember? You don't really want to live in hiding, do you?"

"No," she admitted. "But I would continue to do so to keep you safe."

"We're not beaten yet. I promised to keep you and Hailey safe, and that means getting to the bottom of this mess."

She squeezed his hand, holding on for a long moment before letting go. "Maybe you should check the equipment in case we have to stop and buy replacements."

He grimaced and pulled the duffel bag onto his lap. "I can look for obvious signs of damage, but I won't know for sure until I have a chance to hook everything up."

"Does that mean I should head back to the cabin?" she asked.

"Yeah, for now. We can't plant anything inside the restaurant until after it closes, anyway." Nate poked through the bag, disappointed to see that one of the cameras was clearly broken. But as he peered at the rest of the equipment, everything else appeared intact. He'd brought several cameras, so there was a good chance the others might still function well enough to get the information they needed.

The receivers were the most important part, though, because they really needed the audio feed to understand what they were dealing with.

"Maybe we should find a place closer," Melissa said as she took an exit that advertised cheap gas. "We'll end up spending a lot of money on fuel driving back and forth."

He knew she was right, but he wasn't willing to move locations yet. Tracing the cabin to him would be difficult, so as far as he was concerned, it was their best chance at survival.

He thought back to Melissa's idea of changing their names and disappearing without a trace. It shouldn't have been appealing—after all, being on the run, constantly looking over your shoulder for the threat of danger was no way to live.

But being with Melissa and Hailey once this was over? That sounded way too good to imagine.

Melissa waited inside the car while Nate filled up the gas tank and then went inside to pay with cash. The darkness outside made the hour seem much later than the six o'clock reading on the dashboard.

"Where do you want to eat?" she asked when Nate returned. "I'm sure Hailey will be hungry soon."

"I'm hungry now, Mommy," her daughter piped up.

"Why don't we go inside the pizza joint up the street?" Nate suggested. "I'd like to try and call Jenna to see what happened with those cops outside my house."

"All right," she agreed, pulling back onto the street and heading toward the pizza place Nate had indicated. "Do you think she's in trouble?"

"I hope not," Nate muttered. "Otherwise we're completely on our own."

Melissa swallowed hard and tried not to think the worst. When would this madness stop? Things were spiraling out of control, and now Jenna had risked her career to help them, too.

When she put the car in Park, Nate inserted the battery in his personal cell and powered it up. So much for having those disposable phones. She waited as he made the call, but the phone went to voice mail.

"Jenna, it's Nate. Please let me know you're okay. Thanks." He disconnected from the call and then went through the process of popping the battery back out of his phone.

"What if she tries to call you?" Melissa asked as they slid from the car.

"I'll try again when we're finished eating," he said, opening the back passenger door and unbuckling Hailey from her seat. His actions were rote, leaving her to wonder if he was getting used to traveling with a five-year-old after all.

"Carry me, Mr. Nate," Hailey said when he was about to set her down on her feet.

"All right." He hiked the little girl higher and took her inside. Watching the two of them together caused a funny feeling in Melissa's chest.

"Hailey only likes cheese and pepperoni," she said in an apologetic tone as they approached the counter. "So we'll need to order one half with the works, the way you like it. I'll share with Hailey."

"What if we order everything except onions and anchovies? How about that?" he offered, listing the two items he knew she didn't care for. "We can share whatever's left once Hailey is finished."

"Uh, sure. Thanks," she murmured, placing their order for a large pizza. Once again, she was struck by Nate's easygoing nature. Not that he'd been super demanding back when they'd been together in high school, but she didn't remember him being quite this chivalrous.

She glanced over as he walked Hailey so she could touch the sign hanging from the ceiling outside a mini-arcade. "Look how tall I am, Mommy!"

"Pretty cool," Melissa said, unable to hold back a smile as she watched them together. Whatever had caused him to distance himself earlier seemed to have vanished now.

They took seats at a booth in the corner, and she knew it wasn't by chance that Nate sat so he was facing the door. He dug some quarters out of his pocket and gave them to Hailey so she could play a video game.

When they were alone, Nate spread a napkin out on the table. "Can you draw the interior of the restaurant for me?" he asked. "I need to know the best places to hide the cameras and microphones."

She shook her head. "Nate, I think it's better if I go in and place the devices."

"No way," he said with a frown. "It's too dangerous."

"Give me a chance to explain," she said calmly. "We need to get this right on the first try. I don't know how to use this equipment. You do. I think it's best if you stay outside to make sure the camera and microphones are in a good spot or tell me if they need to be moved. You can test them right away so we'll know they're working."

Nate's scowl deepened, but he seemed to be considering her theory.

"We have one chance to get this right," she added. "We can't afford to mess this up. I worked in that restaurant for two years. I know the nooks and crannies better than you would."

"I don't like it," Nate muttered. "But you have a point. We can't afford to blow this."

Their pizza arrived, so Melissa slid out of the booth to find Hailey. When she returned, she was surprised to find that Nate hadn't started eating yet, as if he was waiting to pray with them.

She urged her daughter in first and then slid in beside her. Melissa bowed her head, but before she could say anything, Nate began the prayer.

"Dear Lord, we thank You for this food we're about to eat and for keeping us safe today. I hope You continue to watch over us as we search for truth and justice. Amen."

Her eyes were a bit misty as she echoed, "Amen."

"Dig in," Hailey chimed in.

"Here, let me help you." Melissa put a slice of pepperoni pizza on Hailey's plate and cut it into small pieces. "Be careful. It's hot."

Nate had piled two slices of pizza on her plate while she was helping Hailey, and she flashed him a grateful smile.

"When did you start attending church?" Nate asked as they enjoyed their meal. Hailey had finished early so they gave her more quarters to play in the arcade.

It wasn't easy to remember the dark days before she'd found her faith. "When I first arrived in California I was scared. Being all alone in a strange city wasn't easy. I worked in a pub serving food, and the only friends I had were other servers. They all liked to party a bit too much, but it wasn't until I woke up in a strange place with a strange man next to me that I realized I needed to pull myself together. While I was walking home, I came across a church."

"Go on," Nate urged, and she was relieved not to see any condemnation in his eyes.

"The bells were ringing, and the sound was so pretty that I stood for several long moments just listening to them. People walked past me, several of them greeting me nicely even though I'm sure I looked terrible." She glanced at him and shrugged. "I can't explain why, but I ended up following a group of people inside. I slipped into a pew in the back and listened to the service. It was as if the pastor was speaking to me directly, although he couldn't have known who I was or anything about me. But when the service was over, I felt as if I'd been given a second chance to do things right."

"I'm glad," Nate said in a low voice. "I hate thinking of how lost and alone you must have felt."

"I was at first, but the church soon became my family."

"Is that where you met your husband?" Nate asked.

"Not then, because I soon realized the bad guys had found me. I packed up and left that very night. But when I arrived in South Carolina, the first thing I did was to join the local congregation, and that's where I met Jeremy."

"I'm happy you found someone, at least for a little while," Nate said. "You deserved to be happy."

"I was happy. Having Hailey was a true blessing." She paused, then continued, "But as much as I cared about Jeremy, he wasn't you."

Nate stared at her for a long moment, a mixture of surprise and attraction reflected in his dark gaze. "I've thought about you often over the years, but I have to be honest. My thoughts weren't always kind."

"I understand." She knew leaving so abruptly, without so much as a word or note, must have hurt him. Especially considering his mother had done the same thing eight years earlier.

"I'm sorry, Nate," she said, reaching out to touch his hand. He surprised her by quickly turning and capturing her fingers in his. "I'm sorry I left the way I did. At the time, I didn't see another way out. But I was young and foolish. I should have trusted in you."

"I would like to think that I would have stood by you

no matter what," Nate said. "But we were both young. Maybe things happened this way for a reason."

She nodded. "God always has a plan. Besides, I can't regret my decisions. If I hadn't left and met Jeremy, I wouldn't have my daughter."

"She's a cutie, that's for sure," Nate agreed. He released her hand and finished his slice of pizza. "I'm going to try Jenna once more, and then we should probably head back to the cabin."

"All right," she said. Hailey came running back and helped herself to more pizza. After eating a second slice, her daughter declared herself full. Using napkins, Melissa cleaned up the girl's hands and face and had boxed up the leftovers by the time Nate returned.

"Still no answer, and no emails, either," he said grimly. "I changed my mind. Let's find a motel room nearby to use while I check out the equipment. No sense in driving another hour out of our way, only to head back into town later tonight. And maybe now our new phones will work."

"Sounds good."

They made their way across the street, where a motel stood opposite from the pizza place. Nate wasn't wearing his uniform any longer, but he still had his badge, which helped them gain rooms without using a credit card.

Soon they were situated in a small but clean room. Melissa kept Hailey occupied with the children's channel while Nate worked, muttering under his breath as he linked items of equipment together. She couldn't help being impressed, especially when he showed her just how it all worked.

"The clarity on these cameras is amazing," she said in awe.

"The listening devices are just as good," Nate said

with a smile. "Looks like we only lost the one camera. Everything else is working fine."

Her gut clenched as she realized this was it. Tonight she'd have to sneak into the restaurant to plant the equipment. "I'm assuming the restaurant still closes at midnight, so what do you think? Should we go at one in the morning? And how will we get in?"

"Yeah, that sounds good. And don't worry, I have my lock-picks. We'll get in." The tone of his voice left no room for uncertainty.

And true to Nate's word, hours later they were back in front of the El Matador restaurant.

She stayed in the car with Hailey who was sleeping, while Nate went over to unlock the back door. Thankfully, someone had shoveled back there so there was no need to worry about leaving footprints in the snow.

It seemed like forever but was really less than five minutes when he returned. "The door is unlocked. Are you ready?"

"Of course," she said, ignoring the way her fingers trembled as she packed the cameras and bugs into the pocket of her hoodie sweatshirt.

"I'll be here, watching everything," Nate said, tapping the laptop computer screen. "Once you get inside, make sure your earpiece works before you do anything, okay?"

"Okay." She opened the door, chanting "I can do this, I can do this" under her breath as she slithered past the putrid dumpster toward the back door of the restaurant.

The years slipped away, everything looking and smelling the way it had when she worked here. The door was ajar, so she pushed it open and stepped over the threshold into the kitchen.

Here things looked different, and she remembered Nate saying they'd updated the appliances and functionality a few years ago. There weren't any lights on inside, but she easily found her way past the counters and into the main dining area.

"Melissa? Are you in there?"

"I'm in," she said softly. "Can you hear me?"

"Yes. Good job."

She didn't feel as alone with Nate's low, husky voice in her ear.

One glance revealed the layout hadn't changed much, except maybe a few more tables added, no doubt as a way to increase revenue. The round table in the far corner was there, and she imagined the mayor and his entourage still used it as their meeting point. There were Christmas decorations, including a garland that framed a picture on the wall behind it.

A perfect spot for one of the cameras.

After she had the first one placed and the listening device nearby, she waited for Nate's approval.

"Looks good. Now get another angle if you can."

Sure, easy for him to say. She managed to find another crevice in the coffee station that faced the table, so she put the second camera there, along with the listening device. She hid the third one near the front door, but decided to put the listening device beneath the round table, for optimal coverage.

"I'm finished," she whispered.

"Nicely done," Nate murmured.

Melissa smiled and nodded as she headed back toward the kitchen. A thud and a crash stopped her in her tracks.

She dropped to the floor, crouching near the coffee station, her heart hammering so loudly she could barely think.

Someone was here!

# ELEVEN

One minute Nate was watching Melissa plant the last listening device on the underside of the table, and in the next he saw her drop like a stone behind the coffee station, glancing around in fear as if something was wrong.

"Melissa? Everything okay?" he asked, feeling his pulse kick up a notch.

She shook her head and pointed behind her, toward the kitchen. What was wrong? Did she hear a noise? The listening devices were designed to pick up local sound, not something from another room.

He'd parked down the road behind the restaurant for two reasons: to stay far away in case there were cops patrolling the area and to make sure the equipment Melissa had planted would work from a distance.

Unfortunately, he was too far away to see the back door. Was it possible someone had slipped inside?

"Did you hear something?" Nate asked in a whisper.

Melissa nodded her head in an exaggerated motion making sure she was in direct view of the camera she'd hidden in the garland around the picture.

"Stay where you are. I'm going to get closer." He glanced back to make sure Hailey was still asleep. She was, but that didn't mean he was comfortable leaving the little girl alone in the car while he went in to investigate.

"Any chance you can get past without being seen?" he whispered. He put the car in gear and made a Y-turn to drive back to the restaurant.

It wasn't easy watching the computer screen and at the same time scanning the area to see if there were other vehicles or people lurking around. But he saw Melissa shrug and then peer around the corner of the coffee station.

Nate pulled into the back of the parking lot, tightening his grip on the steering wheel and hating the fact that she was in danger.

He never should have agreed to let her plant the equipment. How had they been discovered? Were there other cameras inside that he hadn't known about? Nothing else made sense. There was no other way for anyone to know Melissa was inside.

And if that was the case, their cameras and listening devices would be quickly disposed of.

But that didn't matter now. He wanted her safely out of the restaurant. He closed his eyes for a moment, opening his heart to prayer.

*Dear Lord, please keep Melissa safe in Your care. Amen.*

When he finished, he felt calm. "Never mind trying to slip past whoever is in the kitchen. Maybe it's better to get out through the front door," he said in a low tone.

Melissa shook her head again but didn't say anything, so he wasn't sure what she was thinking.

Then she eased around the corner of the coffee station, disappearing from view.

He gently tapped the accelerator, bringing the vehicle closer to the back door without using the headlights, peering through the darkness to see if there was anyone around.

But he didn't see anything out of place. No movement. Nothing.

Was it possible Melissa had imagined the noise?

As the thought formed in his head, the back door edged open, and a short dark figure eased out and ran toward the car. Nate made sure the locks were disengaged so that she could get into the passenger seat.

"Go," she whispered, pulling the earpiece out and dropping it into the console between them.

He was already backing up, just as anxious as she was to get out of Dodge. Neither of them spoke until they were far away from the restaurant.

"What happened?" Nate finally asked, breaking the strained silence.

Melissa let out a heavy sigh. "I heard someone in the kitchen. You didn't see anyone go inside?"

"No, I moved farther down the street," he admitted. "I didn't have a view of the back door. How did you get away?"

"You asked if I could get past them without being seen, so I crept into the kitchen in time to see a tall, dark figure go into the freezer. I took advantage of the moment to slip out."

Nate was impressed with her bravery. "I'm so glad you're okay." He reached over to take her hand in his. "But why would there be someone in the kitchen, anyway? Especially in the freezer?"

"I don't know," she said, holding on to him. "But I'm glad I closed and locked the door behind me when I went inside. At least there was no reason for him to be suspicious."

"Excellent," he said with admiration. "I'm not sure I would have thought of that."

She smiled at him, and his heart squeezed in his chest.

Melissa was different from the girl he remembered from high school.

How was it possible to be even more attracted to her now than he'd been back then? Had to be the adrenaline rush of facing danger, nothing more.

"I wonder if they're using the restaurant for something else," Melissa mused, interrupting his thoughts. "Like drugs?"

He lifted a brow, turning her idea over in his mind. "It could be that one of the workers just came back to pick up something they forgot."

"Except most employees don't have keys," Melissa said in a grim tone. "Maybe I'm prejudiced against this place, but I think there's something more going on here."

"I guess it's possible the person you saw was hiding drugs in the freezer."

She grimaced. "Sounds pretty silly, huh?"

"Not silly at all," he said, pressing on the brakes and executing a U-turn. "Maybe that's the evidence we need."

"We're going back there?" Melissa asked incredulously. "Seriously?"

"I'm going in this time, to check out the freezer," Nate said. "Don't you see? Having hard evidence of a crime can only help us."

"And if you don't find anything illegal in there?" she asked.

He shrugged. "Then we're right back where we started, right? We can listen in on their conversations and monitor them through the cameras, but you said yourself that they were always careful not to say too much in front of the servers. This is a chance we have to take."

"I guess," she said with a sigh. "But be careful, Nate."

"I will." Fifteen minutes later, he pulled onto the street where he'd parked while waiting for Melissa. "Stay here. I'll be back shortly."

"But I can't see the back door from here," she protested.

"I know, but since we don't know for sure if the person in the freezer is still hanging around, it's better that you and Hailey stay out of sight." He paused, pulling out his lock-picking tools. "And if for some reason I'm not back within ten minutes, get out of here."

"I'm not leaving you," she said firmly.

He appreciated her support, but he caught her gaze in the moonlight. "I mean it, Melissa. If I don't come back, get in touch with Jenna and Griff. They're your best shot at being safe if something happens to me."

Her lips thinned, but she didn't say anything more as he slid out of the driver's seat.

"Just remember you promised to be careful," she said just before he closed the door.

He gave her a thumbs-up and moved into the shadows, making his way to the back door of the restaurant. Nate estimated that they'd been gone at least thirty minutes, certainly long enough for the intruder to have left.

The lock wasn't too difficult to get open, and he silently opened the back door, straining to listen. But he didn't hear a sound.

Still, he stepped carefully over the threshold, using a small penlight to show him the way. He wasn't as familiar with the layout of the restaurant, and besides, he'd need light to see what was inside.

The kitchen appeared to be empty. He couldn't be sure that the dining room wasn't occupied, but if Melissa's theory about drugs was correct, there'd be no reason for the guy to stick around.

He silently walked across the kitchen to the giant walk-in freezer, grateful that the overhead light came on automatically as he pried the door open. And just to be sure it didn't close on him, he propped it open with a large box labeled Steaks.

Thankfully, the freezer wasn't too full, but it would still take him time to go through the various containers.

Minutes later, having searched through several boxes of various food items, Nate came across a box labeled Shrimp. But when he looked, there wasn't any seafood inside. Instead, the box was full of bags of white powder.

Cocaine? He pulled out his phone and snapped a picture of the box, then took one of the bags out before closing the box back up.

He wished there was a way to replace the bag with something like flour, but he'd already been in the freezer longer than he'd planned. Nate set the box labeled Shrimp back on the shelf, then left, hiding the bag of what he assumed was cocaine under his sweatshirt.

He held his breath until he was back outside, crossing the parking lot. Headlights pierced the darkness, and he ducked behind the Dumpster, plastering himself against its hard metal side.

Just then, a car pulled into the parking lot, and his instincts screamed at him to stay hidden. Granted, there was a possibility that Melissa was behind the wheel, but somehow he didn't think so.

The vehicle rolled silently across the lot, and when it turned around, Nate could see by the rack with the lights on top that it was a police car.

Sent by the Brookmont chief of police? To protect their drug investment?

Nate went still, all too aware of the fact that he had what was very possibly a kilo of cocaine beneath his sweatshirt. If he was caught, he'd be arrested before he could blink.

He hunkered down, praying that Melissa had caught sight of the police car and had moved along before they had a chance to see her. The last thing they needed was for the officers to get the license plate number, tracing the car back to Jenna. After what had gone down at his house, his colleague was no doubt in enough trouble already.

The vehicle eventually moved on, rolling out of sight, but Nate stayed where he was for several long minutes. For all he knew, the cruiser was parked nearby. Cops working graveyard didn't have nearly the level of activity as other shifts did, and it was entirely feasible that the officers were involved in whatever was going on.

The Dumpster sheltered him from the wind, but the air was still cold, settling deep into his bones. He forced himself to wait a full twenty minutes before edging out from behind the Dumpster.

He swept his gaze over the area, taking his time to make sure that the cruiser wasn't anywhere in sight. He lightly ran to the road, but didn't see Melissa. He was grateful she'd listened to his instructions to stay safe and left.

Although being stranded here alone wasn't exactly a great option either. He tried to figure out which way to start walking, in hopes that Melissa would return to pick him up, when he noticed a car backing out of a driveway.

He held his breath but then relaxed. It wasn't the police cruiser.

It was Jenna's car with Melissa behind the wheel.

He couldn't help but grin at her ingenuity for managing to hide in plain sight. He jogged out to meet her.

Once Nate was settled in the passenger seat, she drove

off, heading in the direction of the interstate. "I take it you saw the police car?" he asked, breaking the silence.

"Yes, just in the nick of time, too," she said, glancing over at him. "I was more worried about you, though. I was afraid they'd catch you leaving the restaurant."

"I was forced to hide behind the Dumpster," Nate admitted. He pulled out the bag of white powder from beneath his sweatshirt. "And I found this in a box labeled Shrimp."

Melissa gasped. "Is that cocaine?"

"I believe so, but we'll need to get it tested for sure. I also took a picture of the other bags in the box." He stuck the bag beneath his sweatshirt again, just because having drugs out in the open wasn't smart on the off chance that they were pulled over.

"So we have evidence that the restaurant is a hub for drug trafficking," Melissa murmured. "Do you think that's enough for your boss to believe us?"

Good question. "Maybe, but I think we should check to see if there is any way to directly implicate the people we suspect are involved."

"And what if they don't go to the restaurant tomorrow?" Melissa asked. "How long do we wait?"

Nate wasn't sure how to answer that. He knew that having the drug evidence along with Melissa's eyewitness testimony should be enough to convince Griff to give Melissa the benefit of doubt. "I'd like to wait until I talk to Jenna, to see what happened at my house after I managed to escape."

"All right, but if we don't hear from her soon, and if we don't pick up anything useful from the listening devices, then we go to your boss, agreed?"

"Agreed." Nate found it difficult to tear his gaze away from her profile. She deserved so much better than this, slinking through the night, hiding from the police. Deep down he trusted Griff, would be willing to put his life, his career on the line to turn himself in to his boss.

But putting Melissa's life in jeopardy was an entirely different matter. He couldn't bring himself to do that.

Not without finding a way to protect her and her daughter if the situation went south.

Their lives were far more important than his.

An hour and a half later, Melissa pulled into the driveway of the lake cabin with an overwhelming sense of relief. It was almost four in the morning, but she was still wide awake.

They'd made it!

There had been so many times when she'd thought for sure they'd be caught, like when that police car arrived. She'd been so afraid, especially for Nate.

"I can carry Hailey inside for you," he offered when she pushed open her driver's side door.

It was crazy, but she absolutely didn't want to touch that bag of white powder. "I'll get her. You have the computer and other stuff to bring in."

He must have understood her apprehension because he didn't argue. He held the door for her, and within minutes she had her daughter tucked into bed.

Nate was in the kitchen, staring down at the bag of cocaine. "I'm not sure where to put this," he said grimly. "I don't really want it in here, yet we need to keep it as evidence."

"What about putting it in a bag and hiding it in a snowbank?" she suggested. "I'd really rather not have that in the house, either."

"All right."

Melissa huddled near the doorway while Nate wrapped

the package up in a couple of plastic grocery bags and took it outside. She noticed he'd buried it to the left of the doorway. Then he returned, closing the door behind him. "We should probably get some sleep. I suspect Hailey will be up bright and early."

"Yeah, that's true." Melissa went over and dropped into a kitchen chair. Despite the exhaustion that weighed her down, the night's adventure would no doubt keep her awake for hours yet. "I know I suggested it, but I never really expected to find drugs," she said in a low voice.

Nate dropped into the chair beside her. "It was a shock to me, too."

"I can't help thinking that the person in the freezer must be an employee at the restaurant," she continued. "Otherwise it's odd that he or she would have a key to get in."

"That's a good point. I wonder who owns it?" Nate asked as he booted up the computer.

Melissa frowned and tried to think back to the time she worked there. She must have known who the owner was, but in her teenage ignorance, she probably hadn't paid much attention.

She leaned over Nate's shoulder, inhaling the woodsy scent of his aftershave, as he searched Brookmont city records for the proprietor. She'd had no idea these types of websites existed, but then again, her job was all about designing them, not searching for data. In her opinion, Nate was trying to find a needle in a haystack.

"Come on, come on," Nate muttered under his breath. He was scrolling through the various screens so fast she began to get dizzy.

Leaving him to his search, she rose to her feet and helped herself to a bottle of water, bringing one over for

Nate, as well. All that nervous energy made her feel as if she'd run a marathon.

"Here we go," Nate said with satisfaction. He took the bottle of water from her, his expression full of gratitude, before he gestured to the name on the screen. "Ralph G. Carter is the owner."

"The name doesn't sound familiar," she said with a frown. "But I wonder what he looks like?"

Nate was already one step ahead of her. He'd typed the guy's name into the search engine, and soon there was a photograph of Ralph George Carter on the screen.

Melissa gasped. "That's him!"

"Who?" Nate demanded.

"One of the men who was at the restaurant that night." She stared at the picture as realization dawned. "They're all in this together."

"So it would appear," Nate agreed grimly. "The pieces of the puzzle are sliding into place."

Melissa hoped Nate was right. The sooner they had the big picture, the sooner she and Hailey could get on with their lives.

Although she couldn't deny that leaving Nate would be difficult. Despite her best efforts, she was becoming emotionally attached to him.

The big question was, did he feel the same way?

# TWELVE

Nate woke up several hours later, groggy and sleep-deprived, as he listened to mom and daughter in the kitchen. He dragged himself upright, feeling guilty for sleeping in when Melissa had been up just as late.

He quickly finished up in the bathroom, then followed his nose to the enticing scent of French toast in the kitchen.

"Good morning," Melissa greeted him. She had her dark hair pulled back in a ponytail, which somehow made her hazel eyes look bigger than usual. "You're just in time for breakfast."

"How long have you been up?" he asked, taking a seat beside Hailey at the table.

"About an hour," she said as she served a platter stacked high with French toast.

"You should have woken me up." She'd got only three hours of sleep, while he'd slept for four hours. "It was my turn to cook."

"It's not a problem. Besides, Hailey was hungry, so I needed to get something going."

Bowing his head, he listened to Melissa's quick prayer and Hailey's inevitable "Dig in" before getting up to grab some coffee.

Caffeine helped blow some of the cobwebs out of his brain. He sat back down and helped himself to a couple of pieces of French toast.

"Can we play outside in the snow again, Mommy?" Hailey asked as she poured a liberal portion of maple syrup over her breakfast. "This time let's make a snow fort!"

"I'm sure we can go out for a while," Melissa agreed.

Nate dug into his meal with gusto, surprised at how hungry he was. Maybe it was because of the events of last night.

Or maybe it was Melissa's cooking. He honestly wasn't used to anyone cooking for him. Not that he could afford to become accustomed to the luxury. He knew that she was making meals for her daughter, not for him personally.

"Have you thought about what our next steps should be?" Melissa asked, interrupting his thoughts.

"I really need to get in touch with Jenna, make sure she's doing okay," he said between bites. "Then I'd like to see if we can pick anything up through the cameras and audio feeds."

Melissa nodded. "Christmas is just four days away," she said in a low voice. "I need to know if we'll be spending the holiday here."

He understood she wanted some sort of celebration for Hailey. "I'll figure out something within the next twenty-four hours," he promised.

Nate knew that they were getting close to having enough evidence to go to Griff. But he wanted as iron-clad a case as possible, especially considering they intended to leverage some very serious allegations against several high-profile community leaders.

A daunting thought.

When he finished eating, he began clearing the table and stacking the dirty dishes in the sink to be washed. Melissa helped, once again adding a strange sort of intimacy as they performed the mundane task together.

He told himself that this wasn't what it would be like to be married with a family. For one thing, he'd be going to work, sometimes on odd shifts.

Which made him wonder what she did to support herself. She must have left a job behind in South Carolina. Was it waiting for her? Or would she have to start over someplace new?

"Do you need my help for anything?" Melissa asked as they finished the dishes.

He flashed her a grin. "Looking to get out of building a snow fort?"

She grimaced. "Maybe. I'm not used to such cold weather."

"Give me a few minutes to check my email and set up the computer cameras. If there's nothing going on, I can play outside with Hailey for a while."

"No need for you to do that," she said, obviously backpedaling. "She's my responsibility, and it's probably better you stay inside to work since I can't search the internet the way you can."

He glanced over at her curiously. "I truly don't mind. I'm sure we can spare an hour or so."

She hesitated, then nodded. "All right."

Nate went over to the kitchen table and opened up his laptop. The cameras were good, but he couldn't validate the listening devices as the hour was still too early for any activity at the restaurant. He logged into his new email account, happy to see a message from Jenna.

I'm okay. The officers were suspicious, but I think I managed to convince them I was on their side. Hope you got everything you needed out of the house.

Nate was relieved she was all right. He quickly typed a response:

We have cameras and bugs planted inside the restaurant. Also found some interesting evidence. Let me know if you have time to meet today.

He sent the email, feeling better about being on the right track. Although he was sure Jenna wouldn't be thrilled to find out that he'd taken potential evidence from the restaurant.

Deciding to cross that bridge later, he closed the laptop and headed over to put on his winter coat, hat and gloves. Hailey and Melissa were already outside, hard at work clearing an area in the snow for the fort.

Hailey was wearing snow pants and boots, but the adults didn't have that luxury. When Melissa's teeth started chattering, he sent her inside.

"I'll hang with Hailey for a while," he said, ignoring the cold dampness of his jeans.

"Thanks. But don't stay out here too much longer," she cautioned him.

"We won't."

Melissa disappeared inside the cabin, and he continued helping the little girl build her fort.

"Are you going to be my new daddy?" she asked.

He felt his jaw drop in shock, and struggled to come up with a good answer. "I think that's something your mom needs to decide," he finally said. "She has to find a man to fall in love with, and once she gets married again, then you'll have a new dad."

Hailey scrunched up her face. "Don't you love my mommy?"

His heart lurched in his chest. "I care about your mom very much, Hailey. We're good friends."

The flash of disappointment in the little girl's eyes stabbed deep. He wanted to make her feel better, but what could he say? Even if he voiced his true feelings for Melissa, he couldn't give the child false hope that they'd all be one big happy family someday.

No matter how much he was beginning to like that idea.

Melissa hung her wet clothes near the heat vents in an effort to help them dry out. When she crossed back over to the window overlooking the front yard, she noticed that Hailey and Nate were deep in conversation.

This was what she was afraid of. Hailey was already bonding with Nate more than Melissa was comfortable with. What would happen when she and Hailey left to go back home? Sure, she could convince herself that her daughter would forget about Nate eventually, but in the meantime, Hailey would miss him.

And so would she.

Melissa gave herself a mental shake and told herself to stop thinking about Nate on a personal level. She was feeling close to him only because he was risking his life and his career to protect her. She'd probably feel the same sense of closeness and gratitude no matter who she was here with.

No, that wasn't true either. For one thing, no one else would have done what Nate had for her and for Hailey.

Plus, Nate had kissed her, rekindling the old feelings that she'd buried a long time ago.

She sank onto the sofa, her knees feeling weak. Was she crazy to fall for Nate? Hadn't she done that already with disastrous results? Not that her leaving twelve years ago was his fault. But she'd meant what she'd said about not regretting the past. Her daughter was a precious gift.

Yet if Melissa were honest, she'd admit that she'd married Jeremy because he was a good, God-fearing man. Not because she was hopelessly in love with him. At the time, she'd believed the feelings she'd experienced with Nate were nothing but silly romantic fantasies.

Being here with him like this made her realize that her feelings for him weren't childish at all.

Although they were definitely romantic.

Melissa leaped to her feet, uncomfortable with the direction of her thoughts. She didn't have time to dwell on her feelings, romantic or otherwise. She strode into the kitchen and put on the teakettle to make hot chocolate for Hailey.

As the kettle warmed on the stovetop, she crossed over to open Nate's laptop computer. There would be a lunch crowd trickling into the restaurant soon. And that meant the staff would be getting ready for their patrons.

She peered at the screen, knowing it wasn't at all likely that she'd recognize anyone from when she'd worked there. But she was soon surprised to see Gayle Flannery, one of her fellow waitresses, making coffee in the large urns. The uniforms had changed over the years, and when Gayle turned around, Melissa could clearly see the silver manager pin on the older woman's lapel.

Melissa sat back in her chair with a frown, wondering just how much Gayle knew about what was really going on at the restaurant now that she was in a manager role. Was the owner, Ralph Carter, keeping her in the dark? Or was she an active participant in the potential drug ring?

Thinking back, she remembered Gayle being a young woman who was attending college in the evening while working the day shift as a waitress. Had Gayle finished her degree? Or had she given up on school?

The front door opened, letting in a blast of cold air as Nate carried Hailey inside. A few seconds later, the tea kettle whistled loudly.

"Ready for some hot chocolate?" Melissa asked, rising to her feet and hurrying into the kitchen to take the kettle off the stove. "Nate, I can make more coffee if you'd prefer."

"Hot chocolate with mini-marshmallows!" Hailey said, waving her arms eagerly.

"That sounds good to me, too," Nate agreed.

"Let's get you out of these wet things," Melissa said, going over to her daughter.

Nate bent over to help at the same time she did, and their heads lightly bumped together.

"Oh, sorry," he muttered, moving out of the way. He followed her example by taking off his damp clothes and spreading them around the heat vents that she hadn't used.

He disappeared in the bedroom while she finished getting Hailey out of her winter clothes. After hanging Hailey's wet things up, too, she poured her daughter a steaming mug of chocolate.

"Be careful," she warned, setting the cup down on the table. "Let it cool off a minute."

Nate returned a few minutes later wearing dry jeans and a navy blue sweatshirt that had SWAT emblazoned across his chest in white. He walked over and helped himself to a mug of hot chocolate, pouring one for her, too.

"Thanks." Why did things suddenly feel so awkward between them?

He nodded and then took a seat behind the computer. "I see you're already watching."

She shrugged. "I recognized one of the employees. Gayle Flannery used to be a waitress on the day shift while I was there. Now she's the manager."

"Interesting." Nate blew on his chocolate and then took a sip. "I wonder how many other employees are still there."

"Probably not many," she said, taking a seat next to him. She looked at the computer screen. Nate fiddled with the controls until they could see both cameras in a split screen format. She leaned forward with curiosity as customers entered the dining area. "Why can't we hear anything?"

"I don't have the volume on yet," Nate said. "I'd rather wait until we have something in particular to listen in on."

"Worried about invading people's privacy?" she asked.

"Yeah, a bit. After all, this isn't exactly an approved undercover operation."

It took a minute for his words to sink in. "So you're saying we can't really use any of this information against them?"

"That's correct. We can't. All we can do is hope to get intel we can act upon."

She tried to hide the sharp stab of disappointment. But then a familiar face caught her eye. "Look! Isn't that your uncle?"

Nate's expression hardened. "Yeah, that's Tom. Seems

like he's at that restaurant quite a bit. After all, we saw his car there last evening, too."

She felt bad for Nate. It couldn't be easy suspecting your own flesh and blood of being a criminal. "Maybe they're meeting so often because of me."

He lifted a brow, the corner of his mouth kicking up in a crooked smile. "Yeah, because of both of us. It just occurred to me that Tom must realize by now we're together."

"Probably, although I guess we don't know for sure what the Brookmont chief of police has told him."

"We're going to find out," Nate said, gesturing to the computer screen. "Randall Joseph, aka Brookmont chief of police, just walked in."

Melissa's stomach knotted when she watched the two men greet each other with terse nods, neither one of them looking very happy. They walked over to their usual table, the one where she'd planted the listening device.

Nate enabled the microphone, but as the men began talking, Hailey interrupted. "Mommy, can we play a game?"

"How about you play your handheld computer game for a while instead?" she suggested, knowing it would be best to get Hailey out of Nate's way. "Come on. Let's sit in the living room."

"Okay," she agreed, scrambling down from her seat at the table.

Melissa couldn't hear what was going on in the restaurant, but once she had Hailey settled on the corner of the sofa, she went back to glance over Nate's shoulder. "Are you getting anything?"

"Not yet," he said with a sigh. "They're being very careful with what they're saying."

Melissa nodded, leaning forward so she could listen in, too.

"Why haven't you found them yet?" the mayor asked in a low voice.

"We're working on it," the police chief replied. "We came close yesterday."

"Close doesn't count," Tom muttered in a harsh tone. "We need to find them today. Top priority. Use more men if you need to."

"That's not as easy as it sounds," the police chief argued. "Sooner or later someone's going to start asking questions."

The two men fell silent as their server approached, asking if they were ready to place their orders.

Melissa looked at Nate. "They're obviously talking about us."

"I know." He scrubbed his hands over his face in a weary gesture. "It's hard listening to them talk about hunting us down."

She couldn't stop from reaching over to put her hand on his. "I'm sorry," she said helplessly. "I wish I'd been wrong about your uncle."

Nate summoned a grim smile. "It's not your fault. So we know they're still looking for us, and we know that they're using the restaurant as a drug drop. But we don't know why they killed Alderman Keith Turner."

"Don't you think it's probably because he found out about the drugs?" she asked. "It only seems logical."

"Yeah, maybe," Nate said, although he didn't sound at all convinced. "But I still feel like there's a piece of the puzzle missing. It's possible Alderman Turner would have gone along with their drug trafficking."

Nate opened a search engine and did more research on

Alderman Kevin Turner. She listened to the conversation in the restaurant, but the men were simply ordering food.

A third man joined them. She recognized him as Ralph Carter, the restaurant owner, but still the conversation remained social.

"That's three, so where's the fourth guy?" Nate asked.

"I'm not sure," Melissa said, unable to tear her gaze from the screen. It was so strange seeing these men sitting at the same table. They all looked a little older, but not terribly so. The police chief had put on about thirty pounds, but the other two men looked very much the same as they had twelve years ago.

"There's a problem with our package," Ralph Carter said. "We're a little short on shrimp."

The three men looked at each other for a long moment. "How is that possible?" Nate's uncle asked.

"I think we have to assume the worst," Ralph Carter said.

Melissa tugged on Nate's arm. "They're talking about the drugs you took from the freezer," she whispered.

He nodded, his gaze focused on the scene at the restaurant.

"I wouldn't have expected him to skim off the top. We pay well enough," Nate's uncle said with a dark scowl. "Are you absolutely sure?"

Ralph's face got red. "Think I can't count? Of course I'm sure. I just checked."

"I'll send a message," the police chief said with an evil grin. "A message our deliveryman won't forget."

Her mouth dropped open in horror. "Oh, no! They're going to do something to that man who placed the drugs in the freezer."

Nate momentarily closed his eyes. "I didn't expect them to discover the missing bag so soon."

Melissa knew they needed the evidence, and she knew that anyone involved in dealing drugs had to be punished, but she wasn't prepared for something like this. The leer on the chief of police's face made her think he enjoyed teaching lessons.

A little too much.

These men had to be stopped and soon. Before more people died.

# THIRTEEN

Melissa's face went pale, and Nate clenched his jaw, hating to see how upset she was.

"We have to do something," she urged him. "If they kill that man, it will be our fault."

Although he understood exactly where she was coming from, there wasn't much he could do. "Melissa, if we knew who the deliveryman was, I'd ask Jenna to arrest him, convince him to talk so that we could place him in protective custody. But we don't." He spread his hands helplessly. "I don't know the name of this guy, and you don't, either."

She sat there for several long seconds, despair shadowing her hazel eyes. "I can't stand the thought that this man will die because we took the evidence from the restaurant."

Nate reached over and held both her hands in his. "Keep in mind that this guy chose to be involved in drug dealing."

Melissa shook her head. "We don't know that. It could be that he stumbled into something and wasn't given much of a choice."

Nate wanted to believe there was always a choice, but thinking back to what had happened to her all those years ago, he could see why she might think that way. Certainly she'd been an innocent bystander whose life had been turned upside down. "You're right," he acknowledged. "Maybe we should try praying for him?"

She lifted her incredibly long lashes to look him straight in the eye, and the hope reflected there made his heart squeeze in his chest. "I'd like that."

It wasn't easy to swallow past the lump in his throat. He took a deep breath to steady himself. Praying didn't come naturally, so he had to concentrate on what he needed to say. "Dear Lord, we ask that You show mercy toward the deliveryman who is currently in danger. Please continue to guide us on Your chosen path. Amen."

"Amen," Melissa echoed.

He couldn't seem to bring himself to release his grip on her hands, as he fought the urge to sweep her into his arms and kiss her. "Mommy, I won! I won the game," Hailey shouted excitedly, breaking into his thoughts.

"That's great, sweetie," Melissa said, subtly tugging at her hands. Nate let her go, instantly missing her warmth.

"Let's play a different game." Hailey tossed aside her computer game and jumped off the sofa.

"How about you draw pictures for us first?" Melissa asked in an obvious attempt to keep her energetic little girl entertained for a while longer. "Mr. Nate and I still have some work to do here."

"Okay," she said before running into the bedroom to get her coloring book and crayons.

There was a small flash in the lower right corner of the computer screen, indicating he had a new message. He quickly checked his email, relieved to see that Jenna had responded.

Evidence? I'm curious. Can't meet tonight, working, but
could meet sometime tomorrow. Let me know when
and where, J.

Nate was disappointed in the delay, but obviously
he couldn't ask Jenna to sacrifice her career for him.
He was doing a good enough job destroying his own
reputation, and he hated to consider what Griff would
think if his boss knew he'd dragged her into this mess.
He racked his brain for a moment, trying to figure out
where they should meet.

Email me tomorrow when you get up. We'll meet at
Caroline's Corner Diner, a halfway point between us,
off Highway 83.

Okay.

Nate minimized the email program and returned to
watching the screen displaying the restaurant. The three
men around the table wore grim expressions on their
faces.

It occurred to him that this would be a good opportunity to check out his uncle's house. The way Tom was
dressed, in a nice suit and tie, it was clear he was working. Was it worth the risk? Would he really find anything of value to their investigation?

"What's wrong?" Melissa asked, her brow puckered
with her frown. "You look upset."

He glanced at her. "Not upset, but I was thinking that
this would be a perfect time to search Tom's house."

She sucked in a harsh breath. "Are you sure that's a
good idea?"

"Not really, but we need to do something." Nate stared

at the men seated around the table again. "It's only a few days till Christmas, but he's clearly working today. This is my best shot at getting in and out without being noticed."

"What if the chief of police has someone watching his home?"

She had a good point. "Jenna's working, but she could still swing by the neighborhood while she's patrolling the streets, to make sure it's safe."

He typed a quick message to Jenna. "And once we know the area is clear, we'll use the same approach we did to get my equipment out of my place. You'll drop me off and then come back later to pick me up."

Melissa didn't look thrilled, but she did nod in agreement.

"We need to get going since it's a long drive to the city." Nate couldn't hide his deep sense of urgency. "I'll have Jenna contact me via our throwaway phones if there's any sign of trouble."

He was glad Jenna responded quickly to his message, agreeing to drive past his uncle's place to make sure there weren't any cops stationed nearby.

When he heard Melissa telling Hailey they were going for a ride, he briefly considered going alone. After all, there was no reason to expose them to further danger.

But before he could voice his idea, Melissa shook her head as if reading his mind. "Don't even think of leaving me here alone without a car and with that…you-know-what hiding in the snowbank. We're coming with you."

There wasn't time to argue. They needed to get back to Brookmont as soon as possible.

But if Nate were honest with himself, he'd admit that he didn't really want to leave Melissa and Hailey behind.

They were a team. Not exactly the same way he and his SWAT teammates were.

But close. Very close. There was a different sort of bond growing between them. And for the life of him, he couldn't bear to do anything that might break it.

Melissa tried not to squirm under Nate's intense gaze, but it wasn't easy. She helped her daughter on with her hat, coat and mittens before drawing on her own winter things.

Nate was standing near the door, with the laptop tucked under his arm, waiting for her. She made sure to grab Hailey's handheld computer game before they headed outside.

Within minutes they were on the road, leaving the cabin behind.

"Are you okay?" Nate asked, breaking the silence that hovered between them.

"Sure." She glanced back to make sure her daughter was preoccupied. "If we're going to be in the cabin over Christmas, I'd like to pick up a couple of gifts for Hailey."

"Okay, we'll do that on the way home," he said. "And we'll decorate the cabin a bit, too."

She was glad he seemed to understand. "Thank you. I'd also like to find a church so we can attend services. I want Hailey to grow up knowing the true meaning of Christmas."

"Shouldn't be too hard to find one where no one will recognize us, although we'll have to stay in the back. I'll search out a couple of options for you when we're finished."

"I appreciate that. Do you attend church on a regular basis?"

Nate didn't answer right away. "A couple of the guys on my team attend one just outside of town, but I haven't been." He paused and glanced at her, a wry expression on his face. "To be honest, I always resisted their efforts to include me in church services."

"Why?"

He shrugged and turned his attention to the highway stretching out in front of them. "Not really sure. Caleb, Declan and Isaac all fell in love with women who believed in God, and I figured they were just going along to keep peace."

She tried not to roll her eyes. "You honestly thought they'd go to church just to make their wives or girl-friends happy?"

"Yeah, pretty much." A defensive note crept into his tone.

"So there isn't a single guy you work with who believes in God and faith?"

"Well, yeah, Hawk—er, Shane Hawkins does. And actually, now that I think about it, Jenna's been going, too." He sent her a sheepish grin. "Guess I've been in denial, huh?"

"Maybe a little," she said with a smile. "But Nate, believing in God and faith doesn't make you weak. It gives you strength."

He nodded, his expression thoughtful. "I don't know that I would have believed that before, but I do now."

Melissa was secretly thrilled he'd admitted it. Out loud. Just like when he suggested they pray for the deliveryman who'd stored the drugs in the restaurant freezer.

"I'm glad," she said. "Because we need all the support we can get."

"That's for sure," he muttered.

The sound of a ringing phone echoed through the car,

and Nate quickly pulled it out and handed it over to her. "Put the call on speaker."

Melissa did as he requested.

"Hello? Nate?" Jenna's voice came over the line.

"Hi, Jenna. I'm here with Melissa. We're on our way to the city."

"Everything looks good. Nothing to worry about at your uncle's house."

"Great. Thanks for letting us know."

"Wait, don't hang up," Jenna said urgently. "You need to know that Griff called me this morning. He told me to report to his office before roll call."

"That doesn't sound good," Melissa said.

"No, it doesn't," Nate agreed. "Jenna, I don't want you to get into trouble over me."

"Yeah, I think it's a little late for that," Jenna said in a dry tone. "You mentioned evidence in your last email."

Melissa found herself holding her breath, waiting for Nate's response.

"Yeah, but I don't think it's enough," he admitted.

"Listen, I think it's time you talked to Griff. The sooner the better. MPD wants your head on a platter, and Griff can't hold them off forever."

Melissa caught the look of surprise that flashed into Nate's eyes.

"He's holding them off?" he repeated, as if he hadn't heard correctly.

"Yeah, but I suspect that's why he wants to talk to me prior to my shift. I think he's already grilled the other guys on the team about where you might be."

A knot formed in the pit of Melissa's stomach. She knew he'd eventually planned to bring what they'd uncovered to his supervisor, but not yet.

Please, not yet!

She wasn't ready and sensed Nate would insist on taking her along. The more she thought about going in, the more worried she became. What if Griff didn't believe her? What if she was arrested? They'd put Hailey into foster care since she didn't have anyone else to take care of her daughter.

"I'll think about it," Nate answered evasively. "I'd like to get more evidence."

"If you wait much longer, you'll be arrested first and questioned later," Jenna said.

"I understand. Thanks."

Melissa pressed the button to end the call, not exactly happy with the reprieve. She sensed Nate truly wanted to go to his boss. And she couldn't blame him for wanting a chance to salvage his career. But she didn't say anything, and they drove the rest of the way without broaching the subject.

When Nate turned down a neighborhood street, she tried to keep her attention focused on the houses they were passing by.

"That one there, the tan brick house with the green trim, belongs to my uncle," Nate said as they rolled past.

She nodded. He drove around the corner, pulling over to the curb directly behind his uncle's place. "Give me twenty minutes," he said as he pushed open the driver's side door. "Maybe head to a fast-food restaurant to get Hailey something to eat."

"Okay. Be careful," she added, hating the thought of leaving him here alone. She awkwardly climbed over the console into the driver's seat and quickly adjusted things for her smaller stature. When she looked outside, Nate was already gone.

She glanced at the dashboard clock, marking the time, before she pulled onto the street.

For a split second, she considered driving away, leaving Nate and the Brookmont murder far behind.

Could she do it? Did he need her anymore? He had the drugs and the cameras. Would her eyewitness testimony really be helpful?

She didn't realize how tightly she was gripping the steering wheel until her fingers cramped painfully. She drew in a deep breath and forced herself to relax.

She drove down the street, turning right at the corner, and then headed toward the chain restaurant they'd passed along the way.

But the idea of taking Hailey someplace safe continued to nag at her.

Unsure of what to do, she tried to open her heart and her mind to prayer.

Creeping into the back door of his uncle's house without being seen wasn't easy. Picking the lock took longer than it should have, but he finally heard the satisfying click as the door opened. Good thing his uncle had never installed the security system he used to talk about.

Nate slipped into the kitchen and paused, making sure no one was home. After a long minute, he proceeded to make his way through the kitchen into the large living room.

The place was immaculate, hardly a speck of dust or anything out of place. He'd been there before, but not in the past few years. For some reason, after his mother deserted them, he and his father had kept their distance from Tom McAllister.

Was he nuts to think he'd find anything to tie his uncle to the drug trafficking here? Probably. Yet he couldn't ignore the urge to poke around a bit.

Nate headed over to his uncle's home office, which

wasn't nearly as tidy as the rest of the house. After sifting through the papers that were on top of the desk, he moved on to the drawers.

There was a file labeled Laredo. Wasn't that a city in Texas? He frowned and pulled it out, noticing that there were receipts from a car rental company located there. Thinking quickly, he used his uncle's printer to make copies of them, wincing at how loud the machine sounded in the silent house.

He folded the copies and stuffed them into the front pocket of his jeans. Nate suspected there was probably more to be found, but since he was running out of time, he headed into his uncle's bedroom.

The master suite was just as neat as the rest of the house, and Nate stopped short when he noticed the photograph sitting on the bedside table. He recognized the laughing woman standing beside his uncle as his mother, Rosalie.

Helpless to resist, he crossed over and picked it up to examine it more closely. The picture had obviously been taken a long time ago, based on how young his uncle looked.

Nate turned the frame over to open the back. People didn't use film as much in this day and age, but they did twenty years ago.

Sure enough, he could see the date printed on the back corner, which coincided with the year of his eighth birthday. The same year his mother left, abandoning him and his father.

For a moment he stood frozen, trying not to relive his painful past.

The photograph on his uncle's dresser shouldn't have been shocking. His uncle claimed to have kept in touch with his mother long after she'd left. Hadn't Tom got the divorce papers signed just a few years ago?

He did wonder though, why didn't his uncle have more recent images of his mother? Or did he have them locked away? If so, why?

Letting his imagination get the better of him wasn't helping. Nate put the picture frame back together, trying to ignore the slight trembling of his fingers. Then he quickly wiped it beneath his sweatshirt to remove any fingerprints before returning it to the bedside table.

A loud thud, sounding very much like the slamming of a car door, roused him from his trip down memory lane. Nate left his uncle's bedroom, his heart thumping loudly in his chest. Through the front window, he could see an older model car in the driveway. A woman dressed casually in jeans and a sweatshirt pulled a large bucket and a pile of rags out of the passenger seat.

It took a minute for Nate to realize his uncle must have a cleaning lady. Without wasting another second, he ducked through the living room into the kitchen, and let himself out the back door. He headed out to the street, glancing up and down for any sign of Melissa. Granted, he was a couple of minutes early, but somehow he'd still expected her to be there waiting.

Nate told himself she'd probably made a trip around the block rather than simply parking there with the car idling. But when one minute ticked by, and then another, he began to get nervous.

He turned and started walking, realizing he was only drawing unwanted attention to himself by standing on the street, obviously waiting for a ride. But with each step he took, dread seeped deeper and deeper into his bones.

Where was she? Had something bad happened? Surely their vehicle hadn't been compromised.

A shiver snaked down his spine. Melissa had listened to Jenna's plea to turn themselves in to Griff. Was that it? Had she decided to drive away, leaving him behind?

She'd agreed they were in this together, but maybe that promise didn't mean much to her. After all, he'd learned the hard way that some women just couldn't be trusted.

His mother's wedding vows hadn't meant anything. She'd had no trouble leaving him and his father behind.

Nate swallowed hard and tried not to think the worst. He desperately wanted to believe Melissa would be here any minute.

Because if she didn't show, he honestly wasn't sure what he'd do next. No matter how angry he would be, he didn't think he'd be able to bring himself to turn her in.

# FOURTEEN

"Hailey, it's time to go," Melissa said for the third time, exasperation lacing her tone. She understood her daughter was tired of being in the car, but they needed to leave.

Now.

"I'm coming," her daughter said in a muffled voice from deep within the fast-food restaurant's play area.

She was contemplating crawling in there herself to drag Hailey out when a cold draft washed over her. She glanced at the door and froze. A Brookmont police officer had walked in.

*Run! Hide!*

Melissa automatically ducked behind the slide, her pulse leaping into triple digits. Was the officer looking for her? Had the police somehow figured out what car they'd been driving?

And what about Nate? Had they found him inside his uncle's house?

She stayed where she was, hoping, praying that the officer would get some food and leave. And when she finally mustered the courage to step out of her hiding spot, she saw him standing at the counter, obviously placing an order.

She took a deep, calming breath. Okay, he was probably just getting a burger, so that meant he wasn't here looking for her. But the very thought of walking past him with Hailey made her knees weak. It was entirely possible that he had a photograph of her with instructions to arrest her on sight.

Or worse.

"Boo!" Hailey yelled, jumping out at her with a mischievous grin on her face.

Melissa yelped, badly startled, which only made Hailey laugh harder.

"I scared you, Mommy!" Hailey crowed between giggles.

"Yes, you sure did." She put a hand to her heart and took a deep breath in a vain attempt to calm her frayed nerves. When Hailey turned to head back into the play area, she quickly caught her daughter's hand. "Oh, no you don't. Playtime is over. We need to go. Where's your coat?"

"Over there," Hailey said, pointing to the far corner, where the garment had been carelessly tossed in a crumpled heap.

Melissa walked over to pick it up, dismayed to realize the police officer had taken a seat right near the door. Did she dare attempt to walk past him with Hailey? Or should she let her daughter play longer?

Nate would be waiting for her to come, so lingering wasn't an option. She'd just have to do her best to act casual.

She helped Hailey put on her coat, zipping it up to her chin. Then she carried her daughter up into her arms, holding the little girl at an angle so that Melissa could cover her own face as they walked past the police officer.

"So, Hailey, what did you ask Santa to bring you for

Christmas?" she asked as they walked past, hoping that the normal conversation would distract her daughter. The last thing she needed was for the little girl to ask where *Mr. Nate* was.

"I want a Cuddle-Me Carrie doll and a new computer game," Hailey said. "Are we going to be home for Christmas, Mommy?"

Melissa almost tripped over her feet in her haste to get outside. "Sure, sweetie, of course," she said as they walked past the police officer. She pushed the door open with her hip but didn't breathe normally until they were safely inside the car and backing out of the parking space.

She cast a quick glance over her shoulder at the cop as they drove out of the lot. Was it her imagination, or was he talking into his radio? No, surely he'd come after her if he was suspicious.

Melissa forced herself to concentrate on the traffic around her rather than worrying about the fact that the officer might be calling for reinforcements. She retraced the route back to where she'd dropped Nate off, driving right past him before realizing it.

Her hands were still shaking from the adrenaline rush, so she simply pulled over and threw the gearshift into Park. Nate jogged over, his expression full of relief.

"I was worried something had happened," he said as he opened the driver's side door.

She managed to get out of the car, but her legs didn't work properly, causing her to stumble against him. Nate caught her up against his chest, concern darkening his eyes.

"What happened, Melissa? Are you all right?"

She tried to nod, unable to speak. She knew she was

overreacting, but the rush of fear overwhelmed basic logic.

Nate simply held her close, waiting for her to calm down. When she tipped her head up to look at him, his mouth was close enough to kiss.

As if he'd sensed the direction of her thoughts, he narrowed the space between them, gently covering her lips with his. His kiss was sweet and gentle.

When he lifted his head, she knew that he'd been just as affected by their kiss as she'd been. But obviously this wasn't the time or the place to relax their guard. They weren't that far from his uncle's house.

"Sorry I'm late," she said, breaking the silence. "It wasn't easy to get Hailey off the play set, and then a Brookmont police officer came in. I wasn't sure what to do."

Nate scowled and quickly glanced around the area. "We need to get out of here."

She was in full agreement with that plan. She pulled away from his embrace and then hurried around to the passenger door. Less than thirty seconds later, they were on the road, putting as many miles as possible between them and the city of Brookmont.

"For a few minutes there, I thought you'd decided to disappear again," Nate said.

She licked her lips and glanced over at him. "I'd be lying if I didn't say that the thought briefly crossed my mind," she admitted. "But I gave you my word that we'd stick together."

"Yeah, I know." Nate's grimace reminded her that he still didn't completely trust her. Because she'd left all those years ago? Or because his own mother had also walked away?

Most likely a combination of both.

But if he had believed she'd broken her promise, why kiss her?

"Mommy, I dropped my game," Hailey said.

Melissa unlatched her seat belt and twisted around to sweep the floor of the car with her hand. She found the game and handed it back to her daughter.

"Now it's my turn to apologize," Nate said once she was settled in her seat. "Obviously trust is something I need to continue working on."

"For me, too," she said. "I know that we have to take everything to your boss, but it's difficult to trust he'll believe in me."

"I'm on your side." Nate reached over and took her hand in his. "And I'll do everything in my power to convince Griff he should be, too."

Melissa nodded, clinging to Nate's hand as if it were a lifeline.

Nate pulled into the parking lot of a crowded shopping mall, belatedly remembering how Melissa wanted to purchase a couple of gifts for Hailey. "I'll hang out with Hailey for a while. You get what you need."

"Thanks. I won't be long."

He caught a glimpse of a coffee shop adjacent to a bookstore that boasted free Wi-Fi. "We'll wait for you over here," he said, gesturing toward the coffee shop.

"Sounds good."

He walked into the building with his laptop under one arm and holding Hailey's hand. She skipped along, obviously full of energy.

"I want to look at the books," she said, tugging impatiently on his hand. "This way, Mr. Nate."

"Okay." How could he resist when her wide hazel

eyes reminded him so much of Melissa's? As much as he wanted to begin investigating the new Texas connection, he allowed Hailey to drag him over to the tall shelves of children's books.

When he caught a glimpse of a children's Bible, he paused and reached for it, thinking that it would be a good gift for him to give to Hailey for Christmas. "Stay here for a few minutes, okay?"

She nodded, her attention already on the picture book she'd found on one of the lower shelves. He listened to her talking, maybe even reading, while he took the Bible over to the closest desk to make the purchase.

It wasn't until he turned back toward the little girl with his new purchase that he realized he didn't have a gift for Melissa. Ridiculous, considering they weren't dating or anything. No reason to think she'd get him a gift. Their holiday celebration was all for Hailey's benefit, nothing more.

The image of the small diamond heart pendant he'd purchased for her back in high school flashed in his mind. Since she hadn't come to meet him that night, he had the necklace buried somewhere in the top drawer of his dresser.

Didn't matter now, he told himself. They were not teenagers anymore. He took a seat at a small table close enough to keep an eye on Hailey and opened the laptop computer. When he activated the cameras, he was disappointed to realize the round table in the corner was occupied by a large family, two parents and three kids. Tom, the police chief and the restaurant owner were gone, most likely back at their respective jobs.

Did they have someone tracking down the deliveryman? Nate hated knowing the guy was in danger all because he'd taken one of the cocaine bags. If only they had a clue as to who he was.

He let his breath out in a heavy sigh, wondering how much longer he'd be able to delay before meeting Griff. The urge to reach out to his boss was strong, but he'd promised Melissa he'd make sure they had a good case with plenty of evidence first.

Nate scrubbed his hands over his face, then turned his attention back to his computer. He searched a bit on Laredo, Texas, located near the Rio Grande, the river that just happened to be the natural separation between Texas and Mexico. A possible drug-trafficking site? Maybe. Drugs were known to come into the US from Mexico. He pulled the rental car information out of his pocket, noticing for the first time that the car hadn't been rented under his uncle's name.

The name on the receipt was Enrique Gomez. Nate knew it to be a common enough Hispanic name that searching for a connection wouldn't be easy.

He was deep in thought when Hailey tugged on his sleeve. "I'm thirsty," she announced.

"Ah, okay. What would you like to drink?"

"I want a cola."

He nodded, reaching for her hand, when Melissa walked up holding a small bag. "No cola," she said firmly, obviously having overheard her daughter's request. "How about we find some chocolate milk instead?"

"Yay, chocolate milk!"

Nate was glad he hadn't already purchased the soft drink. Of course chocolate milk was a better option, but the obvious choice hadn't crossed his mind. More proof that he knew next to nothing about raising kids.

"Find anything?" Melissa asked while they waited in line for their turn.

He shook his head. "A few things. I'll fill you in later."

She lifted her brow and nodded in agreement. Hailey insisted on carrying her milk as they all walked back out to the car, looking very much like a happy family finishing a Christmas shopping trip.

Since meeting Melissa and her daughter, he'd been thinking a lot more about having a family of his own.

His chest tightened as he realized just how empty his life would be once they'd got out of this mess.

Nate cleared his throat and unlocked the car, stowing his purchase beneath his seat. If Melissa noticed his package, she didn't say anything. As they headed out to the cabin, he filled her in on the little bit he'd found at Tom's house.

"Texas, right across the river from Mexico," she echoed with a frown. "Seems odd. I can't imagine why he'd draw attention to himself going down there so often."

"That's just it. The receipts aren't in his name. The driver is listed as Enrique Gomez." He glanced over at her. "Does that name sound familiar?"

Her lips thinned and she shook her head. "Afraid not. No one named Enrique was working at the restaurant while I was there."

He shrugged, knowing it had been a long shot anyway. "The more I think about it, the more I think they must have been in the early stages of their illegal business back then. The fact that my uncle is still in office and the cop you remembered is now the chief of police makes me believe they've been moving up in the world since then. Getting richer and more powerful each year."

Melissa wrinkled her nose. "You're probably right,

but I'm bothered by the fact that they found me after all this time. I find it hard to believe that they've had my father's house staked out since then, too."

"True," Nate said. "Twelve years is a long time. I can't imagine they would have someone watching your dad's house for that long." Then another thought hit him. "Wait a minute. You said you kept in touch with your father over the years, right? That's how you knew he was sick."

"Yes, we kept in touch using Skype. Why?"

"They didn't need someone staking out your dad's house. They only needed a way to hack into his computer."

Melissa gasped. "You really think that's what they did?"

"Yeah, I'm afraid so. It's the only thing that makes sense. Although honestly, if they had done that, I'm not sure why they wouldn't have just gone to South Carolina to find you."

"Maybe they only hacked in recently," she murmured, the corners of her mouth dipping into a frown. "Everyone in town knew my dad was sick, so they may have suspected I'd communicate with him and come home to see him. So much for trying to use a different name and IP address, huh?"

"Don't beat yourself up about this, there's nothing you can do to change it now. We'll just have to be smarter than them moving forward."

She nodded but didn't look entirely convinced. He couldn't blame her. She'd been through a lot since that fateful night.

They made good time getting back to the cabin. Once they were settled inside, he booted up the computer once again, determined to find something to tie his uncle into the drug running.

Not just his uncle, but all three of the men who were there the night Alderman Kevin Turner died. It would be nice to have the identity of the fourth man, but nailing the other three would have to suffice.

With any luck, one of them would turn in the fourth guy for a chance at a lighter sentence.

Searching for Enrique Gomez was like looking for a penny in Lake Michigan. After several attempts, Nate gave up and decided to try another tactic.

Maybe he could use the cameras in the restaurant to make a list of the some of the employee's names who worked there. He wished now that he'd asked Melissa to place one in the kitchen. Then again, he doubted they would be wearing name tags anyway. Still, it was worth a shot.

"Is spaghetti for dinner okay with you?" Melissa asked.

"Absolutely, love it." Once again, a tiny twinge in the area of his heart made him realize how empty his life had been until she'd returned.

"What are you doing?" she leaned over his shoulder, her enticing scent reminding him of her kiss.

"Recording employees, hoping to find one named Enrique."

"I hate to say this, but what if the guy who placed the drugs in the freezer was Enrique?" she asked in a low voice. "He might be the one in danger."

"I know, but I can't very well ask Jenna to track him down when I don't know where to look."

She sighed and straightened. "I'll just keep praying that he survives."

Once he'd recorded as many names as he could, Nate returned to his search efforts. But instead of looking for Enrique Gomez, he typed in his mother's name.

Going back in the newspaper archives, he found several articles and photographs mentioning her name—all of which stopped the year she'd run off on him and his father.

He turned his attention to the Arizona newspapers, looking for any sign of her, without luck. Though that might not mean much, since the average everyday person didn't end up in the newspaper very often.

Nate couldn't get the image of that photograph in his uncle's house out of his mind. A moment frozen in time. He couldn't help feeling as if his mother had disappeared right off the face of the earth.

Or had she died?

No, why would his uncle lie about something like that? Especially about his own sister. For what purpose? To punish him and his father for some egregious action?

With the scent of oregano and tomato sauce simmering in the air, he returned to the Milwaukee area newspapers, searching for information on any Jane Doe investigations.

And hit pay dirt fifteen minutes later.

A young Caucasian woman, in her late twenties or early thirties, with dark hair and a small strawberry birthmark on her shoulder was pulled out of Lake Michigan just south of Gary, Indiana. Unfortunately there isn't enough of her face left to identify the remains. Please call Indiana's Missing Persons Bureau for additional questions.

Nate stared at the date listed at the top. It was three weeks and two days after his mother's disappearance. And she had a strawberry birthmark on her shoulder, too.

A coincidence? Doubtful. A surge of anger mixed with horror washed over him.

Was it possible his mother hadn't voluntarily left him and his father? That she had, in fact, been murdered?

# FIFTEEN

Concentrating on making dinner wasn't easy, every sense Melissa possessed seemed to be aware of Nate. His brief kiss had left her feeling off-kilter, especially because she wanted him to do it again.

Soon.

She glanced over at him, noticing that he seemed to be sitting frozen, staring blindly at the computer screen. Instantly she dropped the spoon she was using to stir the sauce and headed over.

"What's wrong?" she asked, leaning over his shoulder. The woodsy scent of his aftershave was a momentary distraction. She blinked and focused on the computer. She'd expected him to be staring at the cameras located in the restaurant, but instead there was a newspaper article on the screen.

The phrases "Jane Doe" and "dark hair" captured her attention. She bent closer, scanning the short article.

"Gary, Indiana?" she asked.

It took Nate several seconds to answer, and when he did, his voice was rough, as if he could barely get the words out of his throat. "Several hundred miles southeast from Milwaukee."

The realization hit her like a brick to the forehead. "You think this woman might be your mother?"

Nate shrugged, continuing to stare at the computer. "I don't know what to think. All these years, Uncle Tom led us to believe she was alive and well, living in Arizona with some new guy. He'd even got her signature on my dad's divorce papers. Why would he go to all that trouble to lie to us?"

The raw pain in his voice made her heart squeeze in her chest, and she put her arm around his broad shoulders. "If this Jane Doe is your mom, and he did something to her and didn't want you or your dad to investigate it, a lie like this would make sense."

"I can't seem to wrap my brain around it," Nate admitted. He let out a heavy breath and finally turned to look at her, pain and frustration shadowing his eyes. "But you're right. That's the only possible explanation."

"I'm sorry, Nate," she murmured. "After seeing those photographs of your mother with Kevin Turner, I can't help but think Turner was involved in the drug running, and while spending time with him, your mother stumbled upon the truth."

Nate rose to his feet, breaking away from her embrace and pacing the length of the small kitchen. "I can't believe my uncle killed his own sister," he said harshly. "They were so close."

Melissa pressed her lips together, unwilling to point out that Nate didn't really know firsthand that his mother and his uncle were close. For all they knew, that was yet another story Tom McAllister had fabricated to keep Nate or his father from uncovering the truth.

"I'm sorry," she repeated. "We're probably way off base. There's no concrete evidence to prove the Jane Doe found in Gary, Indiana, was actually your mother."

Nate sighed. "Except for the birthmark, my mother had one just like it. It's crazy. I hate knowing my mother might be dead, but at the same time, it's a little comforting to know she didn't leave me and my dad voluntarily. How senseless is that?"

The hint of wistfulness in his tone made her want to comfort him all over again. She curled her fingers over the back of his vacated chair to prevent herself from reaching out to him. "Not crazy at all."

"I'm losing it," he said, scrubbing his hands over his face. "The timing of my mother's disappearance and the discovery of the Jane Doe could be coincidental. Besides, that all happened almost eight years before you witnessed Kevin Turner's murder. Not likely the two events are related."

"Mommy, the food!" Hailey's voice drew her attention from Nate.

Her dinner! Melissa hurried over to stir the sauce, thankful to realize she hadn't scorched it. "Almost ready," she said.

It took another fifteen minutes to make the noodles. Nate had returned to his seat in front of the computer, closing the lid once she announced dinner was ready.

Melissa led a quick prayer, thanking God once again for the meal they were about to eat and for keeping them safe.

"Dig in," Hailey crowed, reaching for her fork.

A hint of a smile tugged at Nate's mouth at her daughter's antics. She couldn't help feeling relieved that he appeared to be getting over the shock of finding the article on the Indiana Jane Doe. For several long minutes, they were all silent as they concentrated on their food.

When they finished the meal, Nate stood up and carried his dirty dishes over to the sink.

"I'll take care of the dishes," she said, jumping up to

join him. "You need to keep an eye on the cameras in the restaurant."

"You cooked," he stated in protest.

She shook her head. "Doesn't matter," she said firmly. "You're making headway on the investigation, more so than I ever could."

He looked as if he wanted to argue, but instead he gave her a hug, so quick that she almost thought she'd imagined it.

"Thanks," he said gruffly. "I owe you one."

No, he didn't. After all, he'd been keeping her and Hailey safe for days now. He'd more than upheld his end of their bargain.

"Mommy, can I watch a movie?" Hailey asked.

She quickly finished washing the dishes, leaving them to air-dry. She wiped her damp hands on the dish towel before turning to her daughter. "Sure, let's see what we can find."

After heading into the living room, she flipped through channels and the cartoon version of *Dr. Seuss' How the Grinch Stole Christmas* flashed on the screen.

"Grinch! I wanna watch the Grinch!" Hailey said, jumping up and down excitedly.

"Okay," Melissa agreed, grateful that the show had just started. She tucked Hailey into the bed, hoping that the little girl might fall asleep afterward.

She left her in the bedroom and headed back into the kitchen. Nate glanced up when she walked in and gestured for her to come over. "I caught a glimpse of a guy named Carlos," he said, showing her the frozen image on one of the split screens.

Melissa sucked in a harsh breath. "I know Carlos," she said. "He was one of the dishwashers back when I was working as a server. Wow, I can't believe he still works there."

"Do you remember his last name?" Nate pressed.

Her heart thudded in her chest. "I can't believe it," she whispered. How could she have forgotten it? "Gomez," she said in a hoarse voice. "His name is Carlos Gomez."

"Is it possible he has a brother named Enrique?" Nate asked with barely repressed excitement.

She cast her memory back to that time in her life. "It's possible," she finally said. "There was an older kid who used to pick him up after work. Could be a brother, or maybe a cousin."

Nate typed in the two names in the computer search engine. "I doubt they lived in Brookmont," he said, half under his breath. "It's too expensive for a restaurant worker. More likely to be commuting from Milwaukee."

"Carlos was a year younger than me," she said. "I remember asking him once because he seemed so young."

Nate nodded without taking his attention from the computer screen. The second stretched into a full minute before he sat back in his seat. "Found him. Enrique Gomez, age thirty. Was caught dealing drugs in Brookmont twelve years ago but copped a plea for a lighter sentence." His grim gaze met hers. "I have to believe these two are related."

She nodded. "Me, too. But which one do you think is the deliveryman? Enrique?"

"Possibly. I'll give Jenna a call, see if she can pull him in for questioning as a person of interest."

"What about Carlos? Maybe you should have her pick them both up, just in case?"

"Not a bad idea," Nate agreed, reaching for his throwaway phone. He tried again, hoping for better luck with the cell service, but then had to switch back to his personal one. "For all we know, they're working this thing together."

She nodded, listening as Nate left a terse voice message for Jenna about the two suspected drug dealers. When he disconnected from the call, he swung back to the computer, typing an email to Jenna, as well. Finally he turned to face her, taking her hands in his.

"Melissa, I think we have enough circumstantial evidence to convince Griff," he said in a low voice. "We should return to the city."

She blanched, wishing she could find the courage to believe in Nate's boss. "You might be right," she said, forcing herself to remain calm. "We can go tomorrow."

Nate's grip on her hands tightened. "Tonight. I think we need to go in tonight."

"No," she protested, yanking her hands from his and jumping to her feet so fast she knocked over the kitchen chair, wincing when it landed with a crash. "It's too late to drive back into the city tonight. Hailey needs a decent night's sleep."

"Melissa," he said again, but she continued walking away, unwilling to listen to any more.

In the bedroom, she glanced at her daughter, who looked as if she were already half-asleep. The Grinch movie was still on, but she suspected Hailey wouldn't stay awake long enough to see Cindy Lou Who save the Grinch from himself.

Her eyes burned with unshed tears at the knowledge that this could very well be their last night together. Anything could happen once Nate turned her in to his boss. If Griff didn't believe her, she could be arrested and thrown in jail, leaving Hailey in the clutches of the foster care system.

The need to run was strong. Her mind spun with

possibilities. Once Nate fell asleep, she could escape in his car, leaving all this behind. Granted, the last thing she wanted to do was to start over again in a new place with a new name. Hailey deserved roots. A home. But at what cost? Not her life.

Melissa never should have promised to stay with Nate. Although really, would it matter if she changed her mind? What difference would it make if he didn't forgive her?

If she gave in to her impulse to leave in the middle of the night, she'd never see him again.

Nate let out a heavy sigh as Melissa stalked away, obviously upset with him. On the one hand, he didn't blame her for wanting her daughter to get a good night's sleep—if that was the real reason for wanting to wait until morning.

But he couldn't shake the feeling that they were running out of time. Ridiculous, because they'd been safe enough here at the cabin. Even if his uncle Tom did a search on his father's new wife, she'd been married before, so her last name didn't match her brother's.

Nate turned his attention back to the cameras planted within the restaurant. The round table in the corner remained unoccupied for the moment. He swallowed a flash of disappointment. Oddly enough, he'd fully expected his uncle and his cronies to gather there again to talk about the crisis of the missing drugs and the fate of the deliveryman.

He went back to his search on Enrique and Carlos Gomez. He discovered Carlos had experienced a run-in with the law, also for possession of drugs. Carlos must not have had enough on him to qualify as a dealer, unlike Enrique, and had been given nothing more than a slap on the wrist for his crime.

Yet being arrested hadn't caused him to lose his job. Most likely because the drugs had something to do with Ralph, his boss at the restaurant.

The two brothers, or cousins, had to be in this thing together. Enrique was obviously the one traveling to Laredo, Texas. Carlos likely had the key to get into the restaurant's kitchen to stash the drugs.

Nate wished he had a concrete way of connecting his uncle Tom to the drug running. Something more than a couple of invoices with Enrique's name on them. They needed something more before they could hand everything off to Griff, his boss. No way could they get a search warrant yet. There had to be more evidence somewhere.

Nate checked his email, but there was no reply from Jenna. No call or text to his cell, either. He told himself that she was busy at work, but the same impending sense of doom wouldn't leave him alone. He kept the battery in his personal phone, just in case she did decide to return his call.

He rose and stretched, fighting exhaustion. He'd had very little sleep since this mess started, so maybe Melissa was right to want to wait until morning to talk to Griff.

Glancing toward the sofa, he decided to stay in the living room for the night. The sofa was too short for him, but that really didn't matter since he couldn't relax enough to get any shut-eye.

He passed the main bedroom, glancing in to verify that Hailey was all right. When he saw that Melissa was packing their small suitcase, he froze, his pulse jumping erratically.

"What are you doing?" he asked in a harsh whisper.

Melissa gasped and jumped around to face him, her cheeks red with embarrassment. And suddenly he understood she was planning to leave.

Tonight.

Sneaking away while he was asleep.

Just as she'd done that first night.

"Packing," she whispered back, regaining her composure.

Gritting his teeth, he walked in, grabbed her hand and tugged, his intention clear.

With a helpless glance at her sleeping daughter, Melissa accompanied him outside the room.

"I can't believe it," Nate said, battling a wave of fury. "So much for your promise not to leave on your own."

Melissa yanked her hand away and crossed her arms over her chest defensively. "What is wrong with packing our things tonight so that we're ready in the morning?" she asked, fire sparking from her hazel eyes.

"Don't lie to me." Nate practically spat the words at her, the sense of betrayal stabbing deep. Logically he knew he shouldn't be surprised. She probably figured that the drugs combined with the truth about his mother's death were enough so that her eyewitness testimony wouldn't be needed. She was wrong, but that wasn't the worst part.

He was hurt, emotionally.

Because he cared about Melissa and her daughter far too much.

"I'm not lying," Melissa argued calmly. "You want to know the truth, Nate? Yes, I was upset. The thought of facing your boss, knowing he could arrest me the moment we meet, scares me to death. Do you think it's easy for me to accept the possibility of Hailey being stuck into the foster care system? Even if we do eventually straighten things out enough to clear my name, my daughter would be alone over Christmas, with strangers who won't love her or care about her the way I do."

Nate could tell she was fighting with her conscience, and the layer of ice around his heart cracked a bit. "Look, I know you don't know Griff, but—"

"You're right, I don't," she interrupted. "And the thought of spending one night away from my daughter fills me with fear."

"Okay, I get it," Nate said, knowing he couldn't quite relate to her parent-child relationship.

Although the idea of never seeing Hailey again once this mess was over caused a flutter of panic.

"No, you don't," Melissa said with a tired sigh. Her shoulders slumped in defeat, and he had to force himself to stay where he was, when all he wanted to do was to pull her into his arms and hold her close.

He struggled to find some sort of compromise. Something that would make her feel better. "What if you dropped me off so I can talk to Griff first, alone?" he asked slowly. "I'll text you to let you know if it's safe to come in or if you should leave."

Hope flashed in her eyes. "Really?" she asked in a choked tone. "You'd really do that for me?"

He didn't want to, but how was that any different from how she felt about presenting herself to Griff? "Yes. I would."

She stared at him for several long moments, as if trying to see into his head. *Good luck with that*, he thought wryly. Even he couldn't make sense out of his thoughts.

"Why?" she asked, breaking the silence. "Why would you do that for me?"

*Because I'm falling in love with you. Again.*

He opened his mouth, closed it and then tried once more. "I couldn't live with myself if you ended up getting arrested," he said, keeping the depth of his feelings to himself. When her eyes widened in alarm, he mentally smacked himself.

"Not that I think it would happen," he added hastily. "I told you before that the sheriff's department has a broader jurisdiction than the Brookmont police do. My boss doesn't answer to them."

"Okay," she said with a tiny nod.

He lifted his brow. "Okay, what?" For some reason, he wanted to hear her say the words.

"I'll drop you off and stay somewhere nearby until you text me one way or the other."

"Good. Then we have a plan," he said, his gaze moving over her as if he could commit her face to memory. As much as he trusted his boss, he couldn't help thinking that there was a slim possibility Griff would demand Melissa be taken into custody. Although he'd already checked to make sure there wasn't an outstanding warrant for her arrest. But that could be only because she'd faked her death. The minute they knew she was alive, things could change.

Facing Griff wouldn't be easy, especially after everything that had happened. Yeah, he had gathered evidence to help prove a full investigation was necessary, but his boss was a stickler about rules, and no way would Nate escape unscathed.

He could only hope that his boss wouldn't suspend him or, worse, fire him. He could survive having a formal reprimand on file, but anything more could seriously impact his position on the SWAT team.

And that was a consequence he couldn't bear to think about.

"Have you heard from Jenna?" Melissa asked, changing the subject.

He grimaced and shook his head. "Not yet." He crossed over to the kitchen table and double checked his email, disconcerted when Melissa followed him.

"No sign of the foursome, huh?" she asked, glancing at the computer screen with a frown. "I'm surprised."

"Me, too," he admitted. "But they were there over the lunch hour, and I'm sure they're trying not to attract too much attention."

"Yeah, right," Melissa said, wrinkling her nose with distaste. "That never stopped them before."

He paused, thinking about that statement. Was the fact that the men weren't hanging out in their usual spot something to be concerned about? Surely they didn't go to the restaurant twice a day, every day?

"Nate?" Melissa's urgent tone jerked him from his thoughts. "Look, headlights."

He leaped over to shut off the nearest light switch, plunging the room into darkness. "Get Hailey and hide," he commanded.

She nodded and disappeared into the bedroom. He pulled his weapon and made his way over to the window overlooking the driveway.

And froze when he realized a dark car had pulled up, blocking them in.

Nate took out his personal cell phone and dialed Jenna's number, nearly falling over in relief when she answered. "The cabin has been compromised," he said in a harsh whisper. "I need backup, now!"

"I'm already on the highway heading west, so I'll take care of it," Jenna promised, disconnecting from the call.

He stuck his phone back into his pocket, peering once more out the window. Two figures emerged from the car. Even in the darkness of the night, Nate could easily recognize his uncle Tom.

Nate swept a frustrated glance over the yard, knowing that they'd easily see the snowman and the snow fort Hailey had worked on over the past two days. And even inside, signs of her presence were everywhere. Hailey's drawings were scattered about, and the board game she had played with her mom was lying on the table in front of the sofa.

He swallowed hard, knowing he'd have to stall at least long enough for Melissa to escape out the back with Hailey. If they were armed, it would be difficult to hold them off long enough for Jenna and the rest of his SWAT team to arrive. Maybe Jenna would call in the local police, but would they believe him, over his uncle?

He had no idea.

Which meant he was on his own.

# SIXTEEN

There wasn't a second to spare. Melissa scooped up their winter gear from the floor near the heating vents on her way into the bedroom. Getting Hailey dressed while the little girl was still half-asleep was no easy task, and she remembered a similar struggle the night she'd sneaked out of the motel room.

"No, Mommy, sleepy," Hailey protested.

"I know, but we have to leave, Hailey." Melissa didn't want to frighten her daughter. The poor child had already been through too much, but they needed to get out of here, now. Before it was too late. "The bad men are here, sweetie. We have to hurry."

Hailey's eyelids opened wide, and Melissa hated seeing the stark fear reflected there. But at least her daughter didn't fight any more, helping to put her arms into the sleeves of her winter coat.

Moments later, she picked Hailey up in her arms and carried her out to the main room. Her heart squeezed painfully in her chest when she saw Nate standing by the window, holding his gun.

"Go out the back. Hurry," he said in a low tone. "I'll hold them off for as long as I can."

Her stomach clenched at the dire expression on his

face. She didn't want to leave Nate here alone, but she couldn't deny the desperate need to keep her daughter safe. What could she do to help? Maybe find a neighbor? It was better than nothing.

With renewed hope, Melissa opened the back door of the cabin, gasping when a cold blast of air hit her in the face. The wind was howling, but she didn't have a choice but to go outside. She ducked her head against the frigid air and quickly waded through the snow, closing the door behind her.

It took a few minutes for her eyes to adjust to the darkness. There wasn't any moonlight, but at least the brightness of the snow provided a nice contrast to the dark cabin and surrounding trees. She hugged the wall of the cabin, inching farther and farther from the back door, trying to decide which way to go.

There were several large pines to the right of the cabin. If she could make it that far without being seen, she'd be in good shape. Of course, there was absolutely no place to hide between the corner of the cabin and the trees.

"Mommy, I'm cold," Hailey whined.

"Shh, I know. Don't talk, okay?" Melissa didn't think her daughter's voice would carry to the front of the cabin, but she wasn't about to take any chances. She hiked Hailey higher into her arms and took a deep breath, preparing to make a run for it toward the safety of the trees.

The idea of running was a joke. Her feet sank deep into the snow, making it difficult to walk, much less move at a fast pace. She didn't even want to think about the fact that she was leaving footprints in the snow behind her. As long as Nate kept the bad guys occupied, the footprints wouldn't matter.

She hoped.

Abruptly a large shadow loomed to her right, and she gasped when strong fingers clamped on her arm. "Gotcha," a deep voice said in her ear.

No! She tried to wrench away from him, but he hauled her more firmly against him and then poked something hard against her ribs.

A gun? She wasn't sure but couldn't take the risk. Not with Hailey.

"Come on. We're going back inside." The stranger tugged forcefully on her arm, leaving her little choice but to obey. It took a minute for her to realize the guy was the same man she'd seen twelve years ago. The man who'd stabbed Alderman Turner outside the restaurant.

A murderer.

Hailey started crying, and Melissa didn't blame her. She wanted to cry, too. But somehow she needed to keep her wits about her.

They weren't beaten yet. Jenna would come to their rescue, right? All they needed to do was to hang on long enough for Nate's teammates to arrive.

As she stumbled toward the cabin, she silently prayed. *Dear Lord, please keep us safe in Your care!*

Nate waited until the door closed behind Melissa before looking for a place to hunker down. The sofa was the best choice, and he quickly dove behind it just seconds before the sound of a muffled gunshot hit the front door. He could hear his uncle Tom and Ralph Carter, the owner of the restaurant, tramping inside.

Nate sat with his back against the wooden frame of the sofa, holding his weapon ready, thankful that Melissa and Hailey had made it out in time. He needed to stay focused, and having two innocent bystanders nearby would only be a distraction.

"Drop your weapons," Nate shouted. "Don't force me to shoot."

"Come on, Nate, you're not going to be able to take out both of us," his uncle said in a calmly detached voice. Nate remained hidden, knowing that his uncle was right. He was trapped behind the sofa, and there were at least two of them. He hadn't seen any sign of Randall Joseph, the chief of police, or the mysterious fourth man, and Nate wasn't sure if that was good news or bad.

He could only pray the other two weren't outside watching the back door. He shook his head against that possibility.

There had to be some way out of this mess.

"I know everything," Nate said, stalling for time. "I know you were part of the group who murdered Alderman Keith Turner. I know you've sent men after Melissa, also known as Meredith, to silence her because she witnessed the crime."

"Listen, Nate, I don't want to hurt you," Tom said in a cajoling tone. "It's obvious you believed that woman's lies, but there's a lot you don't know. She's the dangerous one. She's a drug addict, Nate, and we know that she actually killed the alderman because she needed money for drugs. Trust me, you shouldn't believe anything she says. All we want is to arrest her. The judge can take it from here."

Nate shook his head at his uncle's audacity to try to turn this against Melissa. He knew from the newspaper article that the alderman's body was found in Milwaukee. She'd been right to fear being turned over to the police. No doubt they'd have an eyewitness of their own who would blame the murder on her rather than on the true culprit.

The man they had yet to identify.

"How did you find the cabin?"

"Took a while, but I have resources. Although using your stepmother's family was smart. I'm just glad we got here in time to prevent you from making a big mistake."

His error had been in staying at the cabin for too long. But it was time to switch tactics. "I know my mother is dead," Nate said. "You've been lying to us for years, Tom. She's dead, and I know her death is directly related to the alderman's murder."

There was a long pause, as if he'd shocked his uncle with the depth of his knowledge. Was Tom right now trying to come up with another explanation? Did he really think he and his cronies could simply walk away from this?

There was a loud noise as a door banged open, letting in a cold breeze. Nate's heart sank to the bottom of his stomach long before he heard the words.

"We have the woman and her kid, Nate," Tom said in a harsh tone. "Come out with your hands up where we can see them."

The odds were overwhelmingly stacked against them. He tucked his gun in the small of his back, knowing that it wouldn't take long for the men in the cabin to find it once they frisked him. But since it didn't sound as if they knew for certain he was armed, he figured it wouldn't hurt to bluff.

"Okay, I'm unarmed and coming out," he said in a loud voice, raising his hands over his head. Moving slowly, he rose to his feet and swept his gaze over the room. He could see that Melissa was being held at gunpoint by a tall stranger who he could only assume was the man who'd killed Alderman Turner. Melissa's face was pale, her eyes wide with fear, as she held a sobbing Hailey in her arms.

He hated seeing her being held captive but tried not to let his expression show how helpless he felt. He switched his gaze to his uncle, pondering a way to get to him.

"I know all about the drug running scheme," Nate said in a matter-of-fact tone. "I know you're using Laredo as your point of entry for the drugs and that you're funneling the cash through your respective campaign funds."

The flicker of surprise in his uncle's gaze gave him a small sense of satisfaction.

"Where do you think that kilo of cocaine went?" Nate continued. "I found your stash and turned it over to my boss. In fact, my boss is aware of every bit of evidence I've collected over the past few days. He's probably working on a search warrant for both your house and the restaurant as we speak."

Bluffing his way through this was his only option. Maybe, just maybe, he could keep them alive long enough for Jenna to get here. Or maybe Jenna had already called local law enforcement for help. Either way, he hoped they'd hurry.

"I guess there's no reason to keep him alive, then, is there?" Ralph asked with a menacing scowl. "You were wrong, McAllister. The hotshot cop knows too much."

Nate swallowed hard, knowing that this was the risk he'd taken by being so forthcoming.

"That is regrettable," Tom agreed. "I was hoping to avoid it, but obviously my nephew is too smart for his own good."

"Wait. Before you start shooting, I need you to answer one question for me," Nate said, glaring at his uncle. "I need to know what really happened to my mother. You owe me that much, at least."

His uncle stared at him for several long seconds. "I guess it can't hurt to tell you the truth now." Tom's eyes darkened with grief. "Rosalie was murdered by that no-good jerk she'd decided to sleep with."

Hearing the truth out loud caused Nate to take a shaky step backward. "You mean Keith Turner, don't you? She was having an affair with Alderman Turner."

"Yes, I'm afraid so," his uncle admitted. "She was young and foolish, falling for his pretty-boy surfer looks. I convinced her to break it off before she ruined her future. She agreed and promised to tell Turner that their illicit relationship was over."

"What happened?" Nate pressed, determined to hear every detail.

"I'm not entirely sure. She went missing," Tom said. "I was afraid she'd decided to just walk away rather than confront Turner. So I told your father that she ran off with another man. But then, a few weeks later, a woman was found in Lake Michigan. The minute I heard about the birthmark, I knew the truth. I knew the body was that of my little sister."

"So why keep lying?" Nate asked, truly bewildered. "Why not tell me and my dad that she was dead?"

Tom's expression turned angry. "Because we were searching for her killer, that's why. I suspected Turner but couldn't prove it. Not until years later."

Years? Like eight years? "The night he was stabbed outside the restaurant," Nate said.

His uncle shrugged. "Yes. Apparently your mother found out about our plan to make extra money on the side. Between that knowledge and her determination to break things off and return to you and your father, Turner lost it. He snapped and killed her."

"An eye for an eye," Ralph said with an evil laugh.

And suddenly it all made sense. "You didn't tell my father the truth because you were trying to protect your secret drug business," Nate accused him. "You were afraid the drug running would come out if the authorities dug into the motive for her murder."

Tom lifted his shoulder in an insolent shrug. "It worked, didn't it?"

A haze of fury flashed before Nate's eyes. "You lied to us for years, letting us think she was alive and well and wanting nothing to do with either of us. You didn't even give us a chance to bury her properly. And for what?"

"Enough," Tom said harshly. "Carter is right. You obviously know too much."

Nate ground his teeth together in frustration. "So, what? You're going to kill all of us now? And what's your cover story going to be this time? Lake Michigan is frozen for a good thirty feet along the shoreline. How on earth are you going to explain this away?"

"Murder-suicide, what else?" Carter leered at Melissa, who looked exhausted from holding her daughter for so long. "We'll kill the woman and the kid first, and then you'll conveniently shoot yourself. No one will ever suspect us of any wrongdoing."

"And the evidence that I've turned over to my boss?" Nate asked, trying not to look at the clock on the wall. What was taking Jenna so long? Granted, even going at top speed, Jenna wouldn't get here for a good hour. Was it possible she hadn't called the local authorities for help? "Do you really think the sheriff's department is going to believe a murder-suicide theory when they have the kilo of cocaine and the rest of the evidence we've collected? Not a chance."

Ray's face flushed red and he took a threatening step forward, lifting his gun and pointing it directly at Nate. "You're lying," he said. "If your boss has the evidence he needs, why are you hiding out here?"

"Griff's team is on their way right now," Nate said, maintaining his bluff. He'd been lowering his arms inch by inch, hoping to get a chance to pull his weapon in a last-ditch effort to save Melissa and Hailey. "I just turned over the rest of the evidence a few hours ago."

"I don't believe you," Carter sneered.

"He's telling the truth," Melissa said. "And if you shoot us, the neighbors will hear and call the police."

"Nice try, sweet thing. The houses on either side of you are dark. Nobody home." The stranger holding her spoke up for the first time since dragging them back inside. "We checked the place out. Besides, we'll be long gone before you know it."

"Danny's right," Carter said. "Now, let's set the scene." The restaurant owner glanced between Nate and Melissa. "I like the fact that she's wearing her coat. Looks like she's leaving him, providing a good reason for him to go crazy and shoot her."

Danny? Nate had no idea who he was or his role in all of this, but it didn't matter. He lowered his hands another inch, feeling sick to his stomach. Even if he managed to take out Carter, Danny was still holding Melissa hostage.

There was no way he could put her in more danger. "Tell you what. Let the lady and the kid go, and I'll back your drug scheme. I'm sure you could use another cop on the payroll. Especially one with a wider jurisdiction than the Brookmont area."

"We don't need you," Danny said in a snide tone.

"The Brookmont police department has been handling our needs just fine. Come on. Let's get this done already."

"Now, wait a minute," his uncle said. "Nate has something there. We've been looking for a way to expand our enterprise. We could use someone inside the sheriff's department."

"You're getting soft, old man," Danny accused, waving his gun toward Nate. In these precious seconds, the gun wasn't trained on Melissa. Nate could see that she wanted desperately to move, and he tried to signal her not to do anything foolish with a tiny shake of his head.

"Enough already. We've been here long enough," Carter said. "We'll shoot the woman in the back, as if he'd stopped her from leaving. Then you can shoot him in the temple to make it look as if he killed himself."

Nate was barely listening, knowing he needed to make his move. Now.

He reached behind to grab his weapon at the same time Melissa threw herself to the ground, covering Hailey with her body. He shot at Danny seconds before the sound of another gunshot filled the air.

Nate ignored the searing pain in his shoulder and blood running down his left arm and turned to shoot at Carter, too. Within moments, the two armed men were lying on the cabin floor, while Tom stared at him in horror.

For the first time, he realized his uncle wasn't armed. Foolish mistake on his part. "Get on the ground, now!" Nate shouted at him.

Melissa staggered to her feet and picked up Hailey, running over to Nate's side for safety. "I need you to get the handcuffs from my duty belt. It's in my bedroom, near my uniform," he said to her.

She gave a jerky nod and carried Hailey with her into the spare bedroom, as if she couldn't bear to be apart from her daughter. Not that he blamed her.

Turning back, Nate watched as his uncle slowly lowered himself down and stretched out, giving wide berth to Ralph Carter, who was lying on the floor in a pool of blood. From what Nate could tell, Danny was also severely injured.

He took a cautious step closer, prepared in case Tom tried to make a run for it, when the front door to the cabin burst open. Nate assumed that Jenna's backup had finally arrived, but when he swung his gaze over to the door, he was stunned to realize the man standing in the doorway was none other than Randall Joseph, the Brookmont chief of police.

Nate instinctively fired at the man and then hit the ground, tucking and rolling across the floor to make himself a smaller target. But another gunshot echoed through the room almost simultaneously.

He felt the punch of the bullet hitting his left side, but this time didn't feel the corresponding pain, maybe because he was numb. Nate fired again, catching the police chief high in the shoulder. The man let out a howl as his gun hit the floor. He saw Randall drop to his knees, holding pressure over his shoulder wound.

Seconds later, Jenna barreled through the door, pushing the police chief down onto his abdomen and planting her knee in the middle of his back. "Don't move," she warned, yanking his arms around to the back. "You're under arrest for the attempted murder of a deputy."

Nate wanted to sag with relief. But the room spun wildly around him, and he realized he was losing blood. Too much blood.

"Get an ambulance here, now," Jenna shouted, slapping handcuffs on the police chief. When she finished there, she quickly came over to where Nate was slowly sinking to his haunches.

Melissa hurried out with the second pair of cuffs. She handed them to Jenna, who didn't waste any time in securing his uncle's wrists behind his back.

"Check the other two," Nate ground out, fighting against a wave of dizziness. "Secure their weapons."

"We will," Jenna assured him. Once she finished cuffing his uncle, she headed over to kick the other weapons far out of reach.

Melissa crouched beside him, her eyes wide with fear. "You're bleeding," she whispered.

"It's not too bad," Nate said, even though his vision was getting fuzzy around the edges. There was a fire in his left side, and he suspected he was losing blood at a rapid rate. "Don't leave, Melissa," he begged. "Stay. Make sure they get all the evidence."

Her eyes were full of tears, but she nodded, shrugging out of her coat and pressing it firmly against the oozing wound in his side. "Where's the ambulance?" she cried. "Nate's bleeding badly."

"Don't leave," he repeated, fighting to stay conscious. He wanted to memorize her features just in case she wasn't there when he woke up.

He opened his mouth, trying to tell her he loved her, but he couldn't seem to make his throat work.

Darkness surrounded him.

# SEVENTEEN

Melissa wanted to scream in frustration as she watched Nate lose consciousness. "Hold on," she whispered to him despite knowing he couldn't hear her. She swept her gaze around the interior of the cabin. "Jenna! Hurry!"

Nate's teammate was busy explaining to the local authorities why she needed the two less injured suspects, Randall Joseph, the police chief, and Tom McAllister, the mayor, taken into custody. It was clear the locals weren't sure if they should believe her.

"Contact my boss, Lieutenant Griff Vaughn," Jenna snapped, losing her temper. "We need you to cooperate with us on this."

"Okay, okay," one of the local deputies said. "We'll haul them out of here."

"Thanks." Jenna crossed over to kneel beside Melissa, her blue eyes full of compassion. "Don't worry. Nate's tough. He'll make it."

She knew Jenna was only trying to help, but the blood-soaked ball of fabric beneath her hands told a different story. When the paramedic crew crossed over to the more seriously injured patients first, the two men Nate had shot, she couldn't bear it.

"Nate's a deputy. Shouldn't they be prioritizing his needs first?" she asked Jenna.

Jenna felt along the side of Nate's neck, obviously searching for a pulse. "There's more than one ambulance crew on the way," she said, skirting Melissa's question.

She knew she wasn't being fair, but Nate's life was on the line, too. She glanced helplessly up at Jenna. "There must be something we can do."

Jenna gave a curt nod. "I'll be right back."

Melissa continued to use all her strength to hold pressure on Nate's wound. When she felt Hailey come up beside her, she glanced at her daughter.

"Is Mr. Nate going to be okay, Mommy?"

Tears pricked at her eyes, but she forced a confident smile. "Of course he is, Hailey. Another ambulance will be here any minute."

"I'll help," Hailey offered, placing her small hands over Melissa's. Her daughter's effort to assist only made her want to cry.

Clearly her daughter had grown attached to Nate. And Melissa couldn't blame her.

She'd grown far too attached, too.

She loved him. Not the teenager she'd dated back in high school, but the man he was now.

Her rock. Her partner. Her protector.

"We'll take it from here, ma'am," a male voice said.

She glanced up, surprised to see another ambulance team had arrived. She forced herself to nod, letting go of the pressure she'd been holding over Nate's wound. Moving away from him wasn't easy, but she lifted Hailey, drawing comfort from the way her daughter wrapped her arms around Melissa's neck, hugging her.

She closed her eyes for a moment, sending up a silent prayer that God would heal Nate's wounds. When she opened them, she could see the paramedics had worked quickly, establishing IV access and running in fluids.

It didn't take them long to apply a pressure dressing to Nate's left side and bandage up the wound on his left shoulder.

"Wait. Where are you taking him?" she asked when they bundled Nate onto the gurney.

"To the closest trauma center, University Hospital in Madison," one of them told her.

Jenna stepped up beside her. "I'll take you there," she offered.

"You're not going anywhere, not until I hear exactly what went down." A tall, broad-shouldered man with close-cropped blond hair scowled at them. Melissa could see by his nametag that this was Nate and Jenna's boss, the infamous Griff Vaughn.

A shiver of apprehension skittered down her spine. What if Griff didn't believe her? Although certainly he'd listen to Jenna, his own deputy. Wouldn't he?

"Well?" Griff demanded, crossing his arms over his massive chest. "Start talking."

Melissa darted a glance at Jenna, who didn't seem the least bit intimidated by her boss. "I'm happy to report what I saw," Jenna said calmly. "But most of the action was over by then. It might be better for Melissa to start at the beginning."

Melissa swallowed hard. "Okay, but can we go over to the kitchen? I'd like to give Hailey something to do to keep her busy."

Griff grimaced as he looked at the little girl but nodded in agreement. "Fine."

She needed to believe Nate was getting the best care possible, especially since sitting in the blood-spattered cabin was the last thing she wanted to do. But she understood that the faster she gave the lieutenant her statement, the sooner she could get to the hospital in Madison.

She plopped Hailey in the seat beside her and gave her daughter a coloring book and crayons. "Why don't you draw Mr. Nate a get well soon picture?" she suggested. "We'll take it with us to the hospital."

"Okay," the little girl eagerly agreed.

She noticed the pained expression on Griff's face but wasn't sure what was going through his mind. Did he resent the fact that Nate had got close to her daughter? Melissa took a moment to gather her scattered thoughts. Jenna had told her to start at the beginning, but that meant going all the way back to that fateful summer night.

"Twelve years ago, I witnessed a murder outside the restaurant where I worked, called El Matador." Griff's eyes widened at her blunt statement. "And I've been on the run ever since."

Griff and Jenna exchanged curious glances. "Keep talking," Jenna encouraged her.

Melissa told them about the drugs found in her room, her escape to California, and after she was found there, her move to South Carolina. To his credit, Griff appeared to be listening intently, while Jenna scrawled copious notes on a sheet of paper.

Reliving the past wasn't easy, but Melissa pushed herself to be as calm and factual as possible. When she described the incident at the mall, Griff leaned forward, capturing her gaze with his.

"Deputy Freemont should have come straight to me after shooting the two suspects," he said in a curt tone. "He'll be lucky to have a job when this is over."

Melissa tried not to be intimidated by his gruff approach. "That's my fault," she freely admitted. "I knew there was a cop present the night of the murder, and it turns out he's now the Brookmont chief of police." She narrowed her gaze. "So you'll have to forgive me for not trusting the authorities. After all, they planted drugs in my room to discredit me."

"Go on," Jenna urged her. "Tell us what happened next."

Melissa described their discovery at the Forty Winks Motel and the green van opening fire on them.

"Yeah, I heard from Lieutenant Max Cooper," Griff said, anger etched on his features. "Wasn't happy to hear about it from some stranger rather than directly from my own deputy."

She didn't have a good response to that, so she continued her story, explaining how they'd planted the cameras and bugs at the restaurant. "Oh, that reminds me," she said, leaping to her feet. "I forgot about the evidence."

"What evidence?" Griff demanded.

She went over to the back door and pulled on a pair of Nate's gloves since hers were stained with blood. She darted outside and pawed through the snowbank to the left of the doorway where Nate had buried the cocaine. It took her a while, but she finally found it. She carried it inside, dropping it on the kitchen table in front of Griff. "Nate found this in a box labeled Shrimp in the restaurant freezer."

Griff looked poleaxed. "Is that…?"

"I think so, yes." Melissa explained how Nate had confronted his uncle Tom about the drug running. "Nate discovered receipts that indicate the mayor might be paying Enrique Gomez to fly down to Laredo several times a year. We believe that's the source of the drugs coming into the US."

"Wow," Jenna murmured. "I wonder which cartel they've got themselves involved with."

Melissa was losing patience with this. She wanted—

no, needed—to get to the hospital. "Listen, Nate planned to give you this evidence along with the rest of the information he'd uncovered. But before we could head into town, the men showed up here. I tried to sneak out the back door with Hailey, but some guy named Danny caught me and dragged me back in here. Nate risked his life to save ours. He shot Danny and then Carter, the owner of the restaurant. We thought it was over, but then Randall stormed inside and shot Nate." She paused to take a deep breath. "That's it. That's the whole story. Now can we please go? I need to find out how he's doing."

Griff looked as if he wanted to argue, but Jenna rose to her feet. "Sure, I'll take you right there."

Melissa saw the lieutenant sigh heavily, but surprisingly, he didn't argue. She couldn't wear her coat but saw Nate's jacket flung over the edge of the sofa, so she pulled it on, burying her nose in the fabric and inhaling his woodsy scent.

She couldn't bear to think that he might not make it. Not when they'd just found each other again. Granted, she didn't really know how Nate felt about her. The way he'd begged her not to leave hurt her. It was evidence that he still didn't completely trust her.

And if that was the case, what chance did they have at a future?

Nate blinked, squinting against the brightness shining in through the window. His mouth was Sahara dry, and throbbing pain kept time with his heart.

It took a minute for him to realize he was lying in a hospital bed. His gaze swept over the room, and he became starkly disappointed to find it empty.

He tried to tell himself that Melissa was likely giving

her statement or taking care of Hailey, but he couldn't help but acknowledge their time together was over. She and Hailey were no longer in danger. She had a life of her own down in South Carolina. Yeah, maybe she'd stay through the holiday, if it hadn't passed already.

He started at the clock and then at the calendar on the wall with the dates crossed off, realizing that he'd lost a day. It was already the day before Christmas Eve. How long before Hailey would have to return to school?

Nate shifted in the bed, grimacing as pain stabbed deep. He considered calling the nurse for medication, but the idea of being in a fuzzy haze wasn't appealing. He reached for the plastic cup of water with his right hand, spilling several drops onto his chest as he took a sip.

Gingerly he moved his hand along his left side, feeling the bulky dressing that folded over his torso, covering the gunshot wound. The area was tender, no doubt about it, but he hoped that maybe he'd escaped any damage to his vital organs.

He found himself closing his eyes and thanking God for sparing his life. A sense of peace washed over him, making him realize that while Melissa wasn't here, she'd given him a precious gift.

Faith.

His life would never be the same from this moment on. Somehow he needed to find a way to convince Melissa to give him a chance. And if that meant giving up his job with the SWAT team, then fine.

He'd relocate to South Carolina if he had to.

But first he needed to talk to her. His last memory was seeing her beautiful face hovering over him right before he blacked out. He needed to find out what happened after he'd been taken to the hospital.

Nate used the bed controls to lift himself. Then he

gathered his strength and swung his legs over the edge of the bed while pulling himself upright with his good arm. White-hot pain slashed through him, and beads of sweat popped out on his forehead. Still, he forced himself to sit there for a few minutes, fighting the urge to pass out.

A pretty nurse who looked to be about his age walked into his room, her eyebrows shooting up in shocked surprise when she saw him sitting on the edge of his bed. "Mr. Freemont, what are you doing?"

"Deputy," he ground out between clenched teeth. "Deputy Freemont. And I need to get out of this bed."

"Why? Do you need to use the bathroom?" She crossed over to put a hand on his arm, as if that would prevent him from rising. He suspected that she didn't have the strength to prevent him from doing a face-plant on the floor, so he tightened his grip on the bed rail.

"No," he responded, although now that she'd said it, he discovered it might not be a bad idea to make the trip across the room. "Maybe, yeah. Then I need you to find me a wheelchair. I have to talk to my boss."

He wasn't amused at the way she rolled her eyes. "I hate to tell you, *deputy*, but you're not going to be able to report to work in this condition." She pushed a button on some sort of device around her neck. "Lifting assistance needed in room 18."

Lifting…what? "I can walk there on my own," he said stubbornly. "I just need you to help with that IV machine."

"The macho ones fall the hardest," she said with a sigh, but she obliged him by unplugging the IV pump and rolling it closer. "Ready?"

He wasn't but nodded anyway. He grabbed the IV pole and staggered to his feet. For a moment his knees wobbled like jelly, but then he managed to find his bearings. Walking across the room to the bathroom actually felt good.

He emerged a few minutes later, surprised to find a wheelchair waiting for him. "Uh, thanks," he said, sinking down into the seat.

"Don't go too far," the nurse told him.

Nate nodded, realizing that using his left arm in an effort to propel him forward hurt. He wondered how long it would take Griff to come talk to him. Was his boss still with Melissa? He hoped for her sake that she'd been able to clear her name.

There was a soft rap on his door, and when he saw Melissa hovering there, his heart leaped in his chest. "Hey," he greeted her with a smile. "How are you?"

"That's my line," she said dryly, stepping into his room. There was no sign of Hailey, and he couldn't help wondering where the little girl was.

"You look better than you did yesterday. And earlier this morning," she commented.

She'd been there? His smile widened. "Yeah, well, that's not saying a whole lot, now, is it?"

Melissa's laugh brightened the whole room. "Are you sure you should be up out of bed?"

"I'm sure." His fingers itched to reach out to her, but he forced himself to let her take the lead. "I'm so glad you stayed," he said in a husky voice. "I hope Griff didn't give you too much trouble."

She shrugged and flashed a wry grin. "Jenna protected me in your absence. By the way, one of your buddies picked up Enrique Gomez, and you were right. He spilled the beans about the drug operation for a chance at a lighter sentence."

He nodded, relieved to know the young man hadn't

died because he'd stolen the evidence. "Did we find out who Danny was?"

"Jenna did. She discovered his real name was Daniel Mendez and he's connected to the Mendez-Guadalupe cartel. Unfortunately, Mendez died, but your uncle, the police chief and Ralph are fine. They're not talking, but I think that's just a matter of time."

"Wow, so that's that. Mystery solved," Nate said with relief. "I'm glad that Griff didn't arrest you. I was worried he'd take his anger toward me out on you."

"Has he come to talk to you yet?"

"No, but I'm sure he'll be here soon." Nate wasn't looking forward to that conversation, although oddly enough, he wasn't as uptight about the prospect of losing his job as he had been when this mess started.

"I took the blame for everything," Melissa said, stepping closer.

He was touched by her attempt to shelter him, although in Griff's mind, Nate would still be the one at fault. "Thanks. I appreciate that. But in the end, I own my actions."

Melissa stood there for a moment. Then she reached into her purse to pull out a stack of faded letters. His heart jolted as he recognized them. "I went back to my father's house and found these in a shoe box under his bed," she said softly.

He remembered pouring his heart out to her in those letters and shifted uncomfortably in the wheelchair, hating the way the tips of his ears burned with embarrassment. "Did you read them?"

She nodded, her eyes glistening with tears. "Every single one. You claimed you loved me and would help me through whatever I'd got mixed up in if I'd just come back home."

He nodded, realizing now just how much trouble she'd been in through no fault of her own. "I missed you a lot."

"I missed you, too." Melissa set the letters on the bedside table. "But, Nate, I'm not that same girl anymore. And you're not the same eighteen-year-old boy, either."

Where was she going with this? "Trust me, I'm well aware of how much we've both changed over the years."

She licked her lips nervously. "Hailey was pretty upset when you got hurt."

"I'm sorry she had to see that," Nate said. "Speaking of…where is she?"

"Jenna's keeping an eye on her in the cafeteria."

Nate couldn't imagine Jenna, with her tough-girl attitude, spending time with a five-year-old. For a moment he almost smiled, but then it hit him.

Melissa hadn't brought Hailey into his room, because she was leaving.

She was saying goodbye.

He gripped the armrests of his wheelchair, searching desperately for something to say that might make her change her mind. But then again, he didn't want her to stay out of pity, either.

"Melissa, I want to thank you for showing me the way to God," he said in a low voice. "I know I have a lot to learn, but you've certainly opened my eyes to what is truly important."

Her face filled with joy, making her more beautiful than he'd thought possible. "Oh, Nate! I'm so glad to hear you say that. And I want you to know how much I appreciate everything you did for me and Hailey, too. You risked your life for us."

He couldn't stand it a moment longer. "I love you," he blurted with all the finesse of an elephant charging through a garden. "I know it's probably too soon for you, considering everything you've been through, but I'm begging you to give us a chance."

Melissa's mouth dropped open in shock. "You love me?" she echoed. "I thought you didn't trust me?"

"Of course I trust you. And yes, I love the woman you've become. Your strength. Your faith. The way you interact with your daughter. I love you, Melissa. And I understand Hailey is in school, so if I have to move down to South Carolina, then that's what I'll do." He was willing to promise whatever she wanted in order to keep her.

"What?" Griff's deep baritone rang from the doorway. "You're quitting the team? Since when?"

Nate wished his boss would go away, but instead he bulldozed his way into the room.

"Listen, Lieutenant, I'll give you my statement in a little while, okay? Just leave us alone for a few minutes."

Griff looked taken aback, but Melissa stepped forward and dropped to her knees beside his wheelchair. "Oh, Nate. I love you, too. And I'd never make you choose between me and your career."

Nate let out his breath in a heavy sigh and pulled Melissa up so that he could wrap his uninjured arm around her. "We'll work everything out later," he murmured, completely ignoring Griff, who was pacing restlessly behind her. "Nothing else matters as long as we love each other."

"I know," she whispered back.

He lowered his mouth and kissed her, then buried his face in her hair.

Griff cleared his throat loudly, making Nate groan under his breath. Sometimes his boss could be a royal pain.

"Go away, Griff," Melissa repeated Nate's earlier sentiment. "We need a few minutes alone."

Nate chuckled, then winced as the movement caused some discomfort around his incision. Griff let out a loud harrumph and walked out of the room.

"That's my girl," Nate said with a smile.

She gazed up at him. "He'll be back, I'm sure, so let's not waste a second. Kiss me again, Nate."

"Always," he promised, his heart swelling with love and a renewed hope for their future.

# EPILOGUE

Melissa couldn't believe Nate was being discharged on Christmas morning, but she wasn't going to complain, either. With help from his teammates, his father and Amelia, Melissa and Hailey decorated Nate's house for the holiday, using everything he had stored in the basement.

She'd purchased a gift for him and was nervous about whether or not he'd like the gold watch she'd picked out.

Waiting for Jenna to pick up Nate and drive him home was nerve-racking. Christmas music wafted through the house, and one of Nate's teammates, Isaac had built a fire in the fireplace for them. She'd cooked a hearty chicken soup from scratch in deference to Nate's recent injury. Hailey had been thrilled to find video games stored in the basement, too, and Melissa knew she should feel guilty for using them to keep her daughter distracted.

When Jenna's SUV pulled into the driveway, she took a deep breath and let it out slowly. She opened the door, watching as Nate insisted on walking into the house under his own power.

"Stubborn man," Jenna muttered loudly enough for Melissa to hear.

She couldn't help but smile. Nate's face brightened when he saw her standing there, and he pulled her in for a quick hug. "You're an amazing sight to come home to," he said. Then he swept his gaze over his fully decorated house, including a bright Christmas tree in the corner. "Wow, you've been busy."

"Santa's elves helped," she teased, taking his hand in hers.

Jenna rolled her eyes and crossed over to place a few gifts beneath the tree. Melissa assumed they were gifts from Nate's teammates and was glad they'd remembered him. Jenna moved toward the front door. "I'm heading out since I'm on duty tonight. Call if you need anything."

"Thanks, Jenna." Melissa closed the door behind her, appreciating the female deputy's wry humor.

Nate made his way to the sofa, sitting gingerly in the corner. "My house has never looked this wonderful," he said. "I'm in awe of how you transformed it."

"I wanted you to have a merry Christmas," she said, coming to sit beside him. "Are you hungry? I have soup simmering on the stove."

"Food can wait," Nate said, reaching over to take her hand in his. "Where's Hailey? I think it's time we opened presents, don't you?"

Melissa was surprised but nodded in agreement. "Sure, I'll get her. She found your old video games in the basement. Hope you don't mind."

"Of course not," Nate said, sitting back against the sofa cushion with a sigh. "Man, it's great to be home."

It didn't take long to convince Hailey that opening presents would be more fun than playing video games. The little girl ran into the living room and headed straight for Nate. "You're home!" she said, crawling up beside him and easing herself into his arms, mindful of the injuries Melissa had warned her daughter about.

Melissa's eyes misted as Nate hugged Hailey close, pressing a kiss to the top of her head. "I sure am. It's good to see you, Hailey."

"Mommy said we're opening presents," Hailey announced. "I have one for you."

"I have one for you, too," he said. "It's the one with the snowman wrapping paper."

Hailey didn't waste any time scooting down from the sofa and running to the tree. She picked up her gift and quickly pulled off the gift wrap. "Look, Mommy, a Bible!"

"That's wonderful, Hailey. We'll read the story of Christmas after lunch, okay?"

"Okay."

"Hailey, bring the other present over here, the one with the Christmas tree paper," Nate said. "That one's for your mom."

Melissa glanced at him in surprise. "When on earth did you get that?" she asked, taking the gift from Hailey.

"Open it and I'll explain," he said with a smile.

She opened the small box. Her breath caught at the sight of the small diamond heart necklace nestled inside. "Oh, Nate, it's beautiful."

"That was my high school graduation gift for you," he said. "I'm hoping you'll let me use those diamonds as accents in your engagement ring."

"Engagement ring?" she echoed, wondering if she'd heard him right. "Oh, Nate, are you sure?"

"Come here," he encouraged her, reaching out for her. She scooted over and took his hand in hers. "Melissa, will you do me the honor of being my wife? I promise to love you and to be a good father for Hailey."

"Yes," she whispered, her heart lifting with joy. "Oh, yes, Nate. Of course I'll marry you."

As he kissed her, Melissa knew with a sigh that she was home at last.

\* \* \* \* \*

Dear Reader,

Thanks again for all the letters, emails and Facebook messages you've sent in the past few months about how much you're enjoying my SWAT: Top Cops—Love in the Line of Duty series. It's amazing how you've come to care about my characters as much as I do.

I'm thrilled to present the fifth book in the series, *Holiday on the Run*. I adore writing Christmas books, and this one is no exception. Deputy Nate Freemont is the techno-geek of the SWAT team, but that doesn't stop him from putting his life on the line to protect Melissa, his old high school sweetheart, and her young daughter from danger. Nate becomes determined to put a twelve-year-old murder to rest, especially when he discovers he has a personal connection to the reason behind the crime. But the biggest danger is to his heart.

I hope you enjoy Nate and Melissa's story. I enjoy hearing from my readers. If you're interested in dropping me a brief note or in signing up for my newsletter, please visit my website at laurascottbooks.com. I'm also on Facebook at Laura Scott Books and on Twitter @laurascottbooks.

Yours in faith,
*Laura Scott*

# COMING NEXT MONTH FROM
## Love Inspired® Suspense

### Available January 5, 2016

## SMALL TOWN JUSTICE
*The Defenders* • by Valerie Hansen

Back in her hometown, Jamie Lynn Henderson is determined to help her brother get out of prison. But she'll need Shane Colton to keep her alive long enough to discover the truth: Did her brother really murder Shane's father?

## MOUNTAIN HIDEAWAY • by Christy Barritt

Driven into hiding by her ex's criminal dealings, Tessa Jones is forced to face her past when PI Trent McCabe tracks her down. But as bullets fly their way, Tessa realizes that Trent's her best chance at survival from the killers pursuing her.

## COMPROMISED IDENTITY • by Jodie Bailey

Someone is stealing military laptops containing top secret information—and it's Sean Turner's mission to catch the culprit. When an attempt is made on staff sergeant Jessica Dylan's life, Sean's even more determined to bring down the ring targeting soldiers—and to save Jessica.

## FOUL PLAY
*Navy SEAL Defenders* • by Elisabeth Rees

Nurse Deborah Lewis suspects foul play in the pediatric unit, so security expert Cole Strachan—her ex-fiancé—is called in. But when someone tries to silence Deborah, Cole vows to stop the culprit at all costs.

## THE LITTLEST WITNESS • by Jane M. Choate

After Delta soldier Caleb Judd's nephew witnesses his parents' murders, Caleb hires bodyguard Shelley Rabb to protect the little boy while working to expose the killer.

## FATAL REUNION • by Jessica R. Patch

When Piper Kennedy becomes a suspect in a murder investigation, she has to convince detective Luke Ransom—the man she once loved but was forced to betray—that she is innocent and her life is in jeopardy.

---

# REQUEST YOUR FREE BOOKS!

## 2 FREE RIVETING INSPIRATIONAL NOVELS
## PLUS 2 FREE MYSTERY GIFTS

*Love Inspired®*
# SUSPENSE
### RIVETING INSPIRATIONAL ROMANCE

**YES!** Please send me 2 FREE Love Inspired® Suspense novels and my 2 FREE mystery gifts (gifts are worth about $10). After receiving them, if I don't wish to receive any more books, I can return the shipping statement marked "cancel." If I don't cancel, I will receive 4 brand-new novels every month and be billed just $4.99 per book in the U.S. or $5.49 per book in Canada. That's a savings of at least 17% off the cover price. It's quite a bargain! Shipping and handling is just 50¢ per book in the U.S. and 75¢ per book in Canada.* I understand that accepting the 2 free books and gifts places me under no obligation to buy anything. I can always return a shipment and cancel at any time. Even if I never buy another book, the two free books and gifts are mine to keep forever.

123/323 IDN GH5Z

| | |
|---|---|
| Name | (PLEASE PRINT) |
| Address | Apt. # |
| City | State/Prov. | Zip/Postal Code |

Signature (if under 18, a parent or guardian must sign)

Mail to the **Reader Service:**
**IN U.S.A.:** P.O. Box 1867, Buffalo, NY 14240-1867
**IN CANADA:** P.O. Box 609, Fort Erie, Ontario L2A 5X3

**Are you a current subscriber to Love Inspired® Suspense books
and want to receive the larger-print edition?
Call 1-800-873-8635 or visit www.ReaderService.com.**

\* Terms and prices subject to change without notice. Prices do not include applicable taxes. Sales tax applicable in N.Y. Canadian residents will be charged applicable taxes. Offer not valid in Quebec. This offer is limited to one order per household. Not valid for current subscribers to Love Inspired Suspense books. All orders subject to credit approval. Credit or debit balances in a customer's account(s) may be offset by any other outstanding balance owed by or to the customer. Please allow 4 to 6 weeks for delivery. Offer available while quantities last.

**Your Privacy**—The Reader Service is committed to protecting your privacy. Our Privacy Policy is available online at www.ReaderService.com or upon request from the Reader Service.
We make a portion of our mailing list available to reputable third parties that offer products we believe may interest you. If you prefer that we not exchange your name with third parties, or if you wish to clarify or modify your communication preferences, please visit us at www.ReaderService.com/consumerschoice or write to us at Reader Service Preference Service, P.O. Box 9062, Buffalo, NY 14240-9062. Include your complete name and address.

LIS15

SPECIAL EXCERPT FROM

*Love Inspired*
SUSPENSE

*Driven into hiding by her ex's criminal dealings,
Tessa Jones is forced to face her past when
PI Trent McCabe tracks her down. But as bullets fly
their way, Tessa realizes that Trent's her best chance at
survival from the killers pursuing her.*

*Read on for a sneak preview of*
**MOUNTAIN HIDEAWAY** *by* **Christy Barritt**,
*available in January 2016 from Love Inspired Suspense!*

A bullet pierced the air.

Tessa froze at the sound.

Before she could react, the intruder—this Trent person—dived back into the house and slammed the door. "Get down!"

She must not have been moving fast enough, because he threw himself over her.

"We've got to get out of here!" he grumbled.

She stiffened with alarm at the very suggestion. "I'm not going anywhere with you."

"I promise you that I'm on your side. I don't want to die, either, and if we stay here, that's what's going to happen." He looked at her a moment. "Can you trust me?"

"I don't even know you! Of course I can't."

"You're going to have to decide who you believe in more—me or the men shooting outside your house."

"Neither!" Her answer came fast and left no room for uncertainty.

As a bullet shattered the front window, his gaze caught hers. "Please, Ther—Tessa. I don't want you to get hurt. Your family would be devastated if you were."

Something in his voice seemed sincere, and the mention of her family softened her heart.

"Fine, I'll trust you for now."

"Good. Now we're getting somewhere. Are there any other exits?"

"The basement. We can escape from the storm cellar."

"Perfect. Show me how to get there."

With trepidation, Tessa crawled across the floor.

She reached the basement door and nudged it open. Blackness stared at her on the other side.

"You'll be okay." She heard the whispered assurance from behind her.

He seemed to sense her fear. She nodded again and forced herself to continue.

Another window shattered upstairs. Someone was definitely desperate to kill her.

Trent gripped her arm as they reached the basement floor. He propelled her forward.

"Can you tell me where the stairway that leads outside is?"

"To the right."

With measured motions, he slid the latch to the side and cracked the exterior door open. Moonlight slithered inside, along with a cool burst of air.

There was just enough light that she could catch a glimpse of his breathtaking, although shadowed, features. She spotted his chiseled face, his perceptive eyes, his thick and curly hair.

"How fast can you run?" he whispered.

Her heart pounded in her chest with enough force that she felt certain anyone within a mile could hear it. This could be it. She could die.

*Don't miss*
*MOUNTAIN HIDEAWAY by Christy Barritt,*
*available in January 2016 wherever*
*Love Inspired® Suspense books and ebooks are sold.*

"In spite of what she said, my niece knows I love her, and
she's already beginning to love her family here. Mandy
will adjust soon to the Amish way of life."

"And what about you?"

Leah frowned at Ezra. "What do you mean? I'm happy
to be back home, and I don't have much to adjust to other
than the quiet at night. Philadelphia was noisy."

"I wasn't talking about that." He hesitated, not sure
how to say what he wanted without hurting her feelings.

"Oh." Her smile returned, but it was unsteady. "You're
talking about us. We aren't *kinder* any longer, Ezra. I'm
sure we can be reasonable about this strange situation we
find ourselves in," she said in a tone that suggested she
wasn't as certain as she sounded. Uncertain of him or of
herself?

"I agree."

"We are neighbors again. We're going to see each other
regularly, but it'd be better if we keep any encounters to a
minimum." She faltered before hurrying on. "Who knows?

We may even call each other friend again someday. But until then, it'd probably be for the best if you live your life and I live mine." She backed away. "Speaking of that, I need to go and console Mandy." Taking one step, she halted. "*Danki* for letting her name the cow. That made her happier than I've seen her since…"

She didn't finish. She didn't have to. His heart cramped as he thought of the sorrow haunting both Leah and Mandy. They had both lost someone very dear to them, the person Leah had once described to him as "the other half of myself."

The very least he could do was agree to her request that was to everyone's benefit. Even though he knew she was right, he also knew there was no way he could ignore Leah Beiler.

Yet, somehow, he needed to figure out how to do exactly that.

*Don't miss*
AMISH HOMECOMING *by Jo Ann Brown,*
*available January 2016 wherever*
*Love Inspired® books and ebooks are sold.*